© 2023 Cheryl Denise Bannerman. All rights reserved.

No part of this book may be reproduced, stored in a retrieval system, or transmitted by any means without the written permission of the author.

Print ISBN: 979-8-9854015-5-4
eBook ISBN: 979-8-9854015-6-1

This is a work of fiction. All of the characters, names, incidents, organizations, and dialogue in this novel are either the products of the author's imagination or are used fictitiously.

"Time is a sort of river of passing events, and strong is its current; no sooner is a thing brought to sight than it is swept by, and another takes its place, and this too will be swept away."

~ Marcus Aurelius

Finding Shirlene

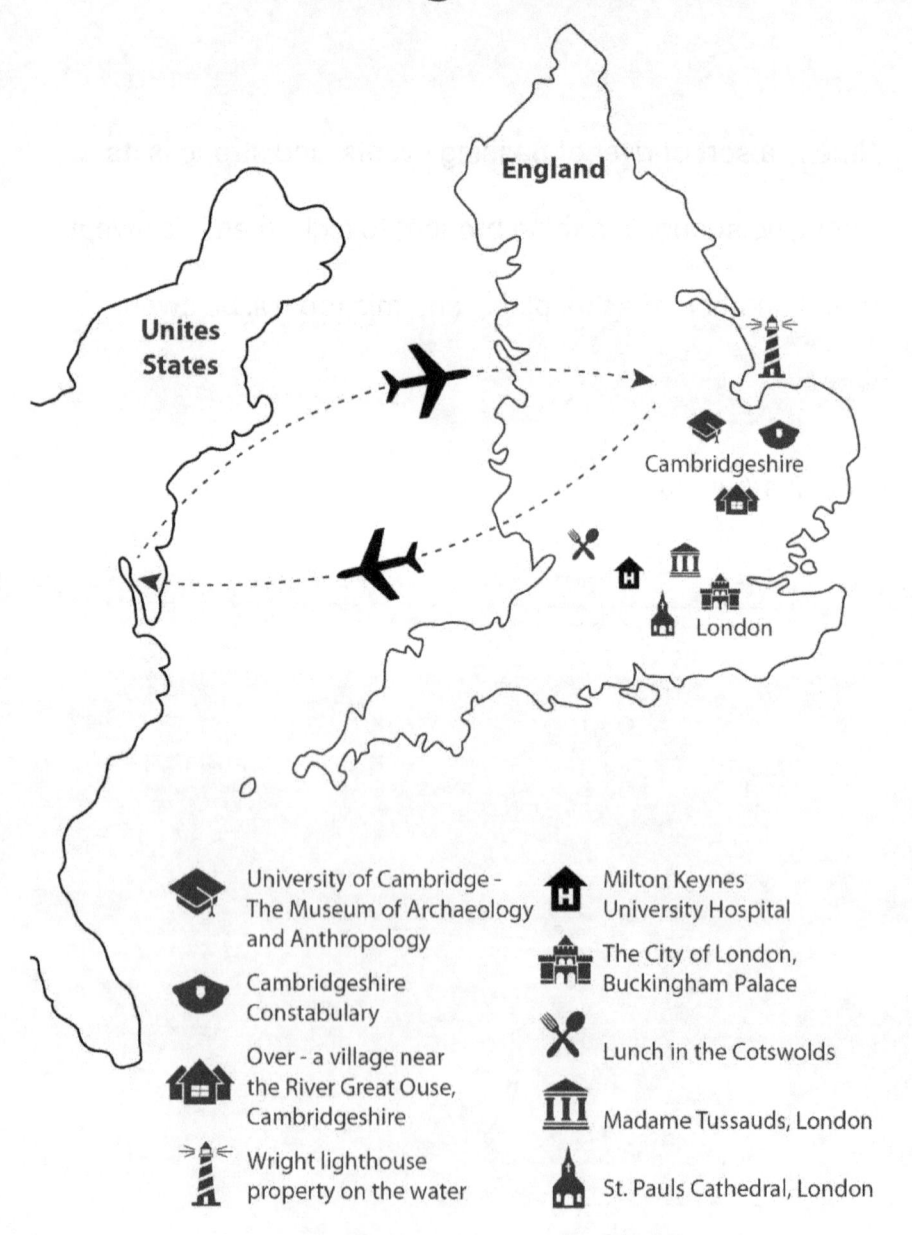

Unites States

England

Cambridgeshire

London

- University of Cambridge - The Museum of Archaeology and Anthropology
- Cambridgeshire Constabulary
- Over - a village near the River Great Ouse, Cambridgeshire
- Wright lighthouse property on the water
- Milton Keynes University Hospital
- The City of London, Buckingham Palace
- Lunch in the Cotswolds
- Madame Tussauds, London
- St. Pauls Cathedral, London

Planes, Trains, and Relics of the Past

An Anna Romano Mystery Series

Book Four

Cheryl Denise Bannerman

Table of Contents

PROLOGUE 7

CHAPTER 1 - An Eye for an Eye... A Snoop for a Snoop 11

CHAPTER 2- All News is Bad News 17

CHAPTER 3 - When Snooping Leads to Souping 23

CHAPTER 4 - To Sir... Without Love 27

CHAPTER 5 - Hawaiian Shirts, Cruise Ships, and Nutty Professors 33

CHAPTER 6 - Making the Connection... Can you hear me now? 40

CHAPTER 7 - My Evil Twin 44

CHAPTER 8 - A History Lesson in Wright and Wrong 49

CHAPTER 9 - Shining Lights and Vacations in Maine 59

CHAPTER 10 - A Major Cliffhanger with a Side of Smelling Salts 65

CHAPTER 11 - Ditching Online Dating for London 73

CHAPTER 12 - Promises of Peace and Pastry Cream Delights 82

CHAPTER 13 - Wedding Bells at the Jersey Shore and Flannel Pajamas 87

CHAPTER 14 - 911 and a Partial Print to Boot 92

CHAPTER 15 - Red Wine and a Blast From the Past 97

CHAPTER 16 - A Case in Question and a Body in Limbo 102

CHAPTER 17 - Jewels, Lies, and Parties on the Beach 108

About the Author 116

Appendix of Tasty Recipes 118

PROLOGUE 1

Anna

I could not believe what the agency just said to me. There had to be some kind of mistake. I sat there on the couch frowning, with my mouth partially agape.

John walked into the room and stopped in his tracks when he saw my face. It was the first Saturday he had off in months and wanted to go out for a special brunch to celebrate our engagement.

"Anna, are you okay? What's wrong?" he asked.

"No one has heard from or seen Shirlene since the day before she left on the cruise. You know Shirlene. She doesn't just NOT answer her phone or texts. I'm afraid something is really wrong, John."

"Now, now, let's not jump to conclusions, rosebud. What do you know about this man she went off with?"

"Nothing really. Just that he's wealthy, handsome and loved to spoil her. I should have pressed her for more information. This is all my fault!" I cried out in desperation.

"This is not your fault. Let me do some digging after we get back from brunch, okay?"

"Brunch. How can you think of food at a time like this? My best friend is missing from a cruise ship!"

"Okay, dear. Email me the cruise ship information and the agency's number, and I'll get right on it. Meanwhile, I'll be in the kitchen making a sandwich."

"Thank you so much, John. What would I do without you?"

I shooed Jasmine from my keyboard and Sonny from my chair and started gathering the information John needed.

After hitting *Send*, I decided to check my email. There were several from the newspaper reminding me to respond to the latest letters from readers who need help with their various personal and professional problems for my Dear Jesse column. And there was one from my mom, wanting to know why she had to hear about my engagement from Bonnie. The last email had no subject, and I was about to drag it to the junk folder when I read the body of the email. All it said was 'Murder at Sea'. It was from a bogus email — just a bunch of numbers followed by "web.net". I froze for a moment, then stood up and trudged to the bookshelf. I looked up at the top shelf and found the book I was looking for. The title was glaring back at me, as if to mock me. *Murder at Sea* by Anna Romano.

It was one of my earlier books when I first started writing and only had two cats. It was about a man who murdered his new bride on the ship and then got off when the ship docked without a trace. He had proposed to the woman on the ship, had a private ceremony performed by the captain, and then created the illusion that she was with him all along by having his accomplice dress up in her clothes. That way, he had witnesses who would attest to seeing them around the ship and getting off the ship together. Meanwhile, the bride was hidden somewhere on the ship in a locked, confined space, and the cops only had seventy-two hours to find her before her oxygen ran out. But the woman in my book was secretly an heir to a family fortune, and he stood to gain a large inheritance if she died. Shirlene doesn't have anything like that, does she? And how would he have known, anyway?

I was reaching up, pulling the book from the shelf, when John walked in with a fried egg sandwich, dripping egg yolk down the front of his shirt.

"What have you got there?" he asked.

"Possibly, the first clue to Shirlene's disappearance."

With a creased forehead, John asked what I meant. I showed him the email and gave him a summary of the book and my thoughts on a possible connection between the plot in the book and what may have happened to Shirlene.

"Okay, Anna, I'm going to stop you right here. This is now officially a suspicious disappearance, and I DON'T want you involved. Understood?"

"But, she's MY best friend, John! You can't expect me to sit back and do nothing!" I shouted. It was the first time I had raised my voice to John, and he was taken aback.

"I know she's your friend. She is a good friend to both of us. Let me take the information you sent me and do some investigating. I've already texted Billings to open a missing person's case for Shirlene. You think you can sit tight for a few hours while I meet with Billings at the station?"

Nodding yes, I plopped onto the couch, reaching for the remote.

"I'll also have the tech guy come over here within the hour to trace the source of the email, so be sure to listen for the door."

I nodded again and turned my attention back to my home improvement show.

The door shut behind him, and my mind quickly switched gears. I was thinking about how to get access to Shirlene's dating site credentials, so I can find out who this mystery man was. There was only one nosy, techy person I knew of whom I could trust to help.

I walked over to the computer, pulled up my messaging app and clicked on her ID, cathym69.

I sat and waited for Chatty Cathy Morton to respond.

CHAPTER 1 |

An Eye for an Eye...
A Snoop for a Snoop

Anna

My nerves were a wreck over Shirlene. I was sitting on the couch with the TV on and flicking the laser pointer back and forth, while Petra and Liza entertained me by chasing it across the room. Just as Sonny was getting in on the fun, my screen dinged. It was Cathy!

> **Cathy:** Hey Big Timer! I see you've been lying low lately. You got a juicy story for me today? Besides the fact that you're hitching up with that handsome detective of yours! What a lucky lady you are!

> **Me:** Well, actually, Cathy, I'm not so good. You know Shirlene, my publicist? Well, she's missing! Went on a trip with this new rich guy and never came back.

> **Cathy:** Oh my word, that's horrible! She is the nicest lady. You let me know if there is ANYTHING I can do to help!

I sat for a minute thinking about what I was about to type and the repercussions. After fifteen seconds, I opted to continue.

> **Me:** Wellllll, there is one thing.

> **Cathy:** Name it! I mean it.

> **Me:** She met this guy on a dating site and I think if I could just get into her account, I could find the guy she went away with.

Cathy: Oh gosh, darling. I'm a snoop for sure, but that 'hacking' stuff is not my area of expertise. Can't your cop fiancé help?

Me: Yeah, sure. I just didn't want to bother him, that's all.

Cathy: Well, one thing I know for sure is people are creatures of habit. It's usually the name of their kids or their pets as their password, mixed up with their date of birth, of course. Does that help?

Me: Absolutely! Thanks Cathy.

Cathy: Wait, so what makes you suspect this guy?

Me: Do you remember *Murder at Sea?*

Cathy: Yeah, sure, you're first book!

Me: Well, the getaway she went on with this guy was a cruise. And the guy was rich, and he met her online!

Cathy: Holy Toledo Anna, that's incredible! I can see why you're worried, especially after the fiasco with that Frederick Talon guy. Promise me you'll keep me posted!

Me: I promise. Thanks again for your advice. Ciao!

I disconnected from Messenger and rushed to the kitchen to set up the feeders for my babies and put out more water. Next, I went to the bedroom to get dressed. I had to get to Shirlene's house and search for her computer. I grabbed my yellow sunflower tee from the drawer, a pair of jeans from the closet, and a light cardigan, just in case. I got dressed and ran to my closet again to slip on my yellow flats, and dashed for the door — snatching my tote bag and keys on the way out.

I was unlocking the car when I heard the familiar humming sound behind me. I let out a deep sigh and said, "Hello, Mr. Craigly," before he could even speak.

"Anna. You heard me coming this time, I see."

I turned around to reply and noticed he was wearing glasses today. "Yes, I did. Are those new?" pointing to his face.

"Stupid doctors, always telling me something else is wrong with me. I see just fine. I knew the light was red. I just didn't feel like waiting. Not my fault cars don't stop for pedestrians."

"Oh, I see. Well, you look very distinguished. I am, unfortunately, on my way out for the day."

"Well, who's stoppin' ya? Geez. You try to be nice to people."

"I'll be sure to bring you a treat later!" I said as I waved and jumped into my car. It seems I had reached a new low with my nosy neighbor. I am now bribing him with treats like my babies. Ha!

Mr. Craigly puttered off, rolling behind my car on the sidewalk just as I put my car in reverse. It was rather tempting, but I waved him along.

It was a long drive to Freehold from Princeton on the New Jersey Turnpike. I dug around in my new tote bag, which happened to be covered in adorable furry cats, for a snack. I found a box of animal crackers and dug in while I tried to find something good on the radio.

An hour and a half later, I was pulling up to Shirlene's house. Her house was more modern than mine. A brown two-story with lots of architectural angles and windows. I would have never pegged her for this type of modern style, because she was such a pragmatic person and very simple in her attire, but here we are.

I remembered the hiding spot for the spare key around back and let myself in. I parked across the street and slightly past her house, just in case I ran into any nosy neighbors.

The back door landed me right smack in the middle of the kitchen. She was a neat freak like me, so every plate, cup, and vase was in its rightful place. On the lower level, I remembered there was a living room, guest room, and bathroom. And upstairs, there were three other bedrooms and two more bathrooms. The master bedroom was hers, then one bedroom was for her exercise equipment, and the third bedroom was her office and library, which were overflowing with books from the floor to the ceiling. I enjoy knowing that I have contributed to that pile.

I smiled and made my way to the upstairs office, where I knew she kept her laptop. However, it wasn't there. I searched the drawers, the floor, the shelves on the wall, and no laptop. The only thing I could find was a tablet in one drawer. I sat down at the desk and powered it on.

"Who are you, and what are you doing here?" a deep voice yelled from the doorway.

I was startled from the chair and quickly slipped the tablet into my tote on the desk in one fell swoop. The officer was reaching for his taser and threatening me to 'put my hands up or else'.

"A neighbor reported a burglary and knows the woman who lives here. And, you're NOT her!"

I explained I was a friend of the owner and who my fiancé was, but the officer ignored me. Next, I was handcuffed and taken outside, where most of the neighbors had gathered in Shirlene's front yard.

"Hey, aren't you that author lady that writes murder mysteries?!" a man in plaid pajamas and an even plaidder robe yelled out.

"Yes, yes, I am. Anna Romano. I'm one of Shirlene's clients," I responded, turning to speak to the officer." You see, officer, this is just a big misunderstanding. If you could call John Solace at the precinct in Hamilton, you'll see."

"Yeah, okay, lady. Just sit right here til I get back."

I sat on Shirlene's front step, smiling at the spectators, and my one fan, while he headed to the squad car to check out my story.

He returned after what seemed to be hours, but was only 20 minutes, and uncuffed me.

"Alright, your story checks out. You're free to go home. Detective Solace told me to tell you to go STRAIGHT HOME. Got it?"

"Yes, sir, officer. Straight home," I said as I rubbed my wrists, which were sore from the handcuffs.

Only my *one fan* waved to me as I walked to my car in shame. What a morning.

My cell phone rang for most of the ride home. I was hesitant to answer it, knowing it was John.

CHAPTER 2 |

All News is Bad News

John

I met Billings at Twenty Volts Café to discuss the case on Shirlene Booker. The smell of coffee beans and bacon filled the air. A line of jittery business people itching for caffeine rocked back and forth on their heels, waiting for their name to be called.

I had almost finished my *double mocha lightning java jolt special* when Billings walked in.

"Morning, sir," he said, rushing over to the table. "Sorry, I'm late."

"Late night?"

"Kinda, sir."

"How are you and Putnam?"

"Okay, I guess. Having a hard time interpreting when she means *yes* and when she means *no*. How do you and Anna get on so well?"

"Well, now, I'm the last person to explain what women want and how they communicate. Especially Anna. But, we have our own system and it just works," I chuckled. "However, if I don't find her best friend, there may not be a 'we' to talk about."

"Yes, sir. Sorry, sir. What have you got so far?"

I filled him in on the details of the case:

> Missing person: Shirlene Booker
>
> Last seen: Fun at Sea Cruise Ship (on a one-week trip to St. Thomas with new boyfriend (unknown))
>
> Notes: Ticket was fully paid for, but by whom, we don't know yet. Ship left from Port Canaveral on Saturday and returned on Friday (same port). Her publishing

agency doesn't know the guy's name and only spoke to her <u>before</u> she boarded.

I let Billings know I already opened the missing person's case and gotten approval from the captain to make the case a priority.

"We should have permission to search Shirlene's cabin soon."

"Great, I'm just going to grab a coffee. Be right back," Billings said.

I was considering a second cup when my phone chirped. A message from Josh, the tech picking up the laptop from Anna. Says no one is answering the door.

I texted back I was on my way and waved for Billings to come over.

"Everything okay, sir?" he asked.

I sighed, shaking my head in disbelief. "Yeah, it seems Anna has disappeared. Josh needs the laptop, and no one is answering the door. I'm going to run over there and get him what he needs, and then meet you back at the station."

"Sounds good, sir."

"Why don't you work on getting a search warrant for Shirlene's home?"

"No problem."

Just then, the barista yelled out, "Billings! Black and sweet!"

Billings headed to the counter, and I headed towards the door. No time for a refill now.

I tried calling Anna on my way to the house, but it went to voicemail. Where could she be?

I pulled up behind Josh, waved, and apologized for the inconvenience.

"No worries, sir. Happy to get out of the office for a change!" he exclaimed.

"I'm sure. Come on in," I gestured as I held the door open. "Watch the cats. Make sure they don't make a run for it."

I walked towards the desk where the laptop was and brought up the history from this morning. Just as I suspected. Anna was into something. Not only was she trying to find out how to get into Shirlene's dating site account, but she was also chatting with none other than Chatty Cathy. I rubbed my eyes and shook my head, sighing again.

"Everything okay? You have another migraine, sir?" Josh asked, knowing I was prone, and they were a hazard of the job.

"I'm fine. Here's the laptop. Let me know if you need anything else."

Josh took the laptop and left, almost disappointed I had got him what he needed so quickly. We should get him out in the field more often.

A moment later, my phone rang.

"Solace!" I barked.

"Yes, is this Detective John Solace?" the caller asked, as if unsure who he was calling.

"Yeah, this is him?"

"This is Officer Wilkins, sir, from the Freehold police department. Your precinct transferred me."

"Oh, okay. How can I help you, Officer Wilkins?" I replied with a furrowed brow.

As he explained he had Anna in custody for 'breaking and entering' at Shirlene's home, my migraine quickly spread to that spot right between my eyes and my left eye began to twitch.

I explained the missing person's case to him and who Anna was in my friendliest voice and asked if he could release her into my custody.

The officer said he would do me a professional courtesy and let her go, and I promised to watch her more carefully.

I was already planning the speech I was going to give Anna when I spoke to her. But for now, I had to grab a bottled water and down a few aspirins. My head was killing me.

I was locking up and heading to the precinct to check in with Billings when my phone chirped again. There were two messages.

The first message was from the captain wanting to know what was going on with Freehold police and Anna, and the second message was from Billings to tell me the captain was yelling to himself about me in his office and that the warrants came in.

I pushed the phone button next to his name to call him back while looking in the mirror at my eye. How do I get this twitching to stop? Maybe I should consider retirement.

"Thanks for calling in, sir. Captain is pretty upset. Just thought you should know."

"Yep. What else is new. The warrants, Billings?"

"Yep, looks like the home search will have to wait. The warrant for Shirlene's cabin on the ship is ready and we have to hurry because it's set to leave port tomorrow."

Looks like Billings and I will need to fly out to Port Canaveral in Florida right away. I'll take a second to pack a bag and call Anna on the way.

Since I would be away, I messaged the captain asking for a patrol car to be placed outside my home while I was away. I couldn't have Anna getting into any more trouble trying to find her friend. She will just have to sit tight and trust I am doing everything in my power to find her. She is a good friend to both of us.

Next stop, meet Billings at his apartment and head to Newark International Airport.

I dialed Anna from the car, waiting for her voice to fill the speakers, but my calls still went straight to voicemail. I left her a message updating her on the case and where I was headed.

I didn't bother telling her about the police car outside the house. And we'll have to talk about her 'criminal activities' when I get back.

I turned up the soft rock radio station and turned on the siren to beat the traffic. Billings and I had a ship to catch.

CHAPTER 3 |

When Snooping Leads to Souping

Anna

Traffic was sluggish on the Turnpike, and my body was dying to get out and stretch. Despite my 'almost arrest', it was a bright, sunny day, and I had at least achieved something during my morning B&E. I patted the tablet tucked safely away in my tote bag and smiled.

My phone chime alerted me there was a voicemail waiting for me. Even the chime sounded ominous, as if it knew I was in trouble. Ha!

I connected the bluetooth to my car speakers, pressed the button to dial my voicemail, and turned the volume up on the radio so I could hear. John's voice echoed throughout the car.

I sat upright when I heard his message. There was a break in Shirlene's case! Thank God!

He and Billings were headed to Florida to search her cabin before the ship leaves the port. They finally got the warrant and the local police had it taped off until their arrival.

I had almost missed my exit for Princeton. His last words to me were, "Billings and I are on the case and we'll find her. I'll call if we find anything. And Anna, I need you to stay put. Okay? Promise me you'll stay put."

I disconnected, already forgetting what John had asked, and thought about my friend. It's a horrible feeling not knowing if someone you love is alive or... somewhere hurt... or worse. I tried to catch the anxiety in my throat as I choked back the first of many tears to come. Wiping my eyes with a tissue, I assured myself she was okay, telling myself to stay positive, and hoping this tablet provides some type of clue where she was or who took her.

I was finally pulling onto my street. There was a patrol car sitting across the street from my house. I wonder what that's about.

I waved at the officer as I got out of the car and headed inside. Petra and Bette were fighting over the automated mouse toy, while Liza watched from the cat tower like a judge in a tennis match.

Tiny was the only one who greeted me with head rubs against my leg and loud purrs.

Who knows where the rest of the crew were hiding.

After a quick bathroom break, I grabbed a bottled water and started working on the tablet from the couch. It was locked with a password. Luckily, it only took me three tries to crack. How about that? It was the name of Shirlene"s late German shepherd, who was her baby for ten years, plus her birth year.

Photos was the first folder I spotted on the desktop, so I opened it. There were just a few pictures of Shirlene with a man I did not know, but his face was partially hidden in each one. He had wavy, silver hair, a dress shirt with shiny cufflinks, white slacks, and a navy blazer embossed with the initials EW. This must be the guy she was talking about who took her on the cruise.

I hate to say it, but Shirlene never looked happier. Seeing her smile like that made me think I was blowing this whole 'missing' thing out of proportion. Maybe she just wanted to be alone with her new man. But, when I thought about it again, I knew Shirline would never abandon her friends or her career, and not respond to messages. Her phone was her lifeline, and publishing was her life.

There was no email set up on her tablet, and I could not find one dating app she had downloaded.

Planes, Trains, and Relics of the Past

Next, I went into the browser and searched the history. I squinted to make sure I was seeing correctly. How odd. My friend, who hates anything related to history or geography, seems to have a new interest in valuable relics from England for some odd reason. I guess she could have been doing research for one of her authors, but that wasn't really like her.

All this research is making me hungry. I whipped up a pot of Pasta Fagioli soup. I pulled my large saucepan out of the bottom cabinet and started cooking my sausage over medium heat.

Sipping my soup and cradling my bowl in my hand, I returned to the couch to finish my snooping. Otherwise known as research. Ha!

It seems this particular collection of artifacts contains both Christian and pagan symbolism, and were carried as talismans into battle and worn as battle gear. It was discovered hidden somewhere in England.

This is all so bizarre. What does any of this have to do with the mystery man or Shirlene's disappearance? Maybe he was from England? Or maybe he just works in a museum, or is an archeologist? Ugh. This was going to be a long night.

Jasmine and TatorTot curled up next to me on the couch as if they could sense my frustration and sense of dread. Thank goodness for my babies.

CHAPTER 4 |

To Sir... Without Love

Planes, Trains, and Relics of the Past

Sergio Wright

It was never supposed to go this far. To complete the collection, I just needed the other piece of the relic. Then I can claim what was rightfully mine. I was told as a young boy about the relics in our family's history and was fascinated.

I had fond memories of playing hide and seek on the grounds of the castle with my mother, and it often caused a slight catch in my throat. But the tears would never come. Father never allowed such expressions from his only son.

Mother and I would spend hours running in the vivid green grass, having picnics, and rolling down the endless hills. This was the only time we could be free, when father was at work. Once the 'king' was in the castle, all behaviors, body movements, and facial expressions went rigid to match the 'cold as ice' exterior of Sir Wright. This is the name father insisted we call him. It was a sign of the utmost respect.

Ricardo Wright was born into money and made his living in investments, turning his inheritance into a living fortune. He was known as the 'broker for England's wealthiest.' He spent his free time traveling the world acquiring rare archeological treasures, which took him away from home more often than mother would have liked.

An arranged marriage brought Ricardo and Isabella, my mother, together in holy matrimony. A year later, I was born into the empire. I was raised by my mother mostly, but always had a nanny, maid, or cook a stone's throw away in case mother was otherwise occupied.

Private tutors provided my earlier education, except for that time father sent me off to boarding school. Before I left, things were the worst between my parents. Constant bickering echoed through the halls of the castle, as if they were atop the highest peak of the tallest mountain.

I wrote to my mother every day about the horrid teachers and the other boys in my dorm and how I longed to come back home.

After four semesters, Father allowed me to return, yet he was more strict and cantankerous than ever. My mother and father didn't speak much anymore, so the distant echos in the hallways were filled with the soft lull of classical music from the radio in the servant's quarters.

I was a teenager by then and had my own friends I'd met from the town's Cricket games and the local pub hangout a mile away. The pub catered to the rich kids on the 'castle' side of town and offered great food, a few arcade games, two pool tables, and a dartboard for entertainment.

I also noticed since coming home, Mother wasn't home as much. She had joined the woman's socialite group and played bridge on Thursdays and Saturdays. But, we still set aside time on Friday nights to watch movies together in the parlor and stuff ourselves with Parmo, Walkers Worcester Sauce Crisps, and Jaffa Cakes. Our cook, Grace, made the best Parmo, deep-fried in breadcrumbs. The chicken cutlet was covered in a creamy, three-cheese sauce, and topped with bacon and a special garlic sauce. I cherished those times.

It wasn't long after that she passed from a rare form of cancer in the lymph nodes.

Throughout the rest of high school and my years studying criminal justice in college, I strived to make my mother proud, and dedicated each honorary award to her name.

It was in my final year of college, during a holiday break with Father, that he broke the news to me. The treasured relics and all the wealth and power promised to me would be split with a half-sister in the States I never knew existed. Apparently, my mother had an affair and Father could not bear to raise another man's child, so they sent the child away. Now, planning for his final days, my usual coldhearted father sent one of the pieces to her and changed his will. Why choose now to shed his ice exterior in Mother's name?! Why? For a random act of kindness to a child he abandoned? And how come I never received any of that kindness? He's never once even told me he was proud of me, or came to one of my award ceremonies at school, or even said he loved me!

I was silent the rest of the holiday, exchanging pleasantries, but could not wait until I could return to university and never see his stern, judgmental face ever again. And no matter what he 'says' happened, I will NOT allow him to taint my mother's precious memory. That bastard! I sat on the train back to school seething, thinking of a way to correct the injustice that was done to me. I've waited my whole life to inherit what's mine. How could he?

After graduation, at twenty-two years of age, I stood at his bedside as he took his last breath. The heart the doctors had tried to save twice before had finally frozen over.

Seven years later, I had formulated my plan to right his wrong. Working in the justice system had allowed me to come in contact with many unsavory characters. And I found just the right con man to help me complete my mission. His name was Ernest Williamson, a rather handsome lifetime criminal with a seedy past, who could charm the pants off any woman.

After years of searching, I found her–my illegitimate sister. Her name was Shirlene Booker. Once the plan was in motion, she fell head over heels with Ernest and getting her on the ship was simple.

As if on cue, Ernest's name appears on my caller ID.

"What is it?"

"Uhhh, I got some bad news, boss," he stammers.

"What now, Ernest? Don't tell me you don't have the relic yet!"

"I still can't find it, boss. But you'll be happy to know Shirlene is locked up tight in our usual meet-up spot and will never be found."

"You brought her here?! Why wasn't I informed of this? Did you take the private jet?" I exclaimed.

"Of course, yes. And, before you ask, no flight plan was logged."

I could tell he was smiling proudly on the other end of the phone, and for no reason. He had no idea what kind of hell I was about to unleash on him.

"You listen to me, you idiot! I need that relic to complete the collection! I'm paying you a lot of money to carry out this plan and if you can't deliver, I'm going to take back more than just my money! Understood?"

"Yes, sir! I completely understand. I have an associate in the States as we speak going to the ship to search her cabin again."

"Imbecile! You better hope he can be trusted and that he finds that relic!"

I hung up fuming without another word and summoned the valet to pull my car around. I had to head towards the 'meeting spot' and make sure the 'package' Ernesto delivered was locked up tight. Anyway, it was about time I met this annoying threat face-to-face.

CHAPTER 5

Hawaiian Shirts, Cruise Ships, and Nutty Professors

John

Anyone else would be happy to have a job that whisked them away to Florida at a moment's notice, but not me.

This was a serious case involving a close friend, so there was no time for fun-in-the-sun. Anyway, I hate the humidity in Florida. My shirt was sticking to me as soon as I got off the plane. Meanwhile, Billings is like a kid at Disney, gawking over the palm trees, pretty women, and ocean waves. He and Anna would be quite the pair sunning-it-up in Florida. With their bright yellow sunglasses, sun visors, Florida tee-shirts, and sunblock on the tips of their noses like true tourists.

The ride service dropped us off at Port Canaveral and we walked towards the massive cruise ship. The captain waved us onboard from the main deck in full uniform with a welcoming smile, even though the circumstances did not warrant such joy.

I greeted the captain as I removed my suit jacket and wiped my forehead with the back of my hand. Billings was chuckling because he changed his clothes on the plane and donned a bright Hawaiian shirt with white linen pants.

"Welcome to Florida! Miss Booker was in cabin 108. Right this way, detectives."

A large gentleman by the name of Smalls guarded cabin 108. I was told he was normally the bouncer for the nightclub on board. He stepped aside and opened the door for us to enter. The captain stepped in after us.

"Geez, sir! Looks like the place has already been tossed!" Billings shouted.

"I assure you, no one has been in this room since we docked. I just don't understand," replied the captain.

Furniture was overturned, white pillow stuffing from the couch cushions spilling out from what looks like slashes from a knife, drawers yanked out of the dresser and thrown about, a cracked TV screen on the floor, and opened cabinets with the contents strewn. Someone was definitely in looking for something valuable.

I was astonished and agitated at the same time. With no CSU to document evidence or look for forensic clues, *since it was not an official crime scene*, we were searching for clues in the dark. I didn't see many of Shirlene's personal items visible, except for some clothes, one flip-flop, and a makeup case on the bathroom counter. From what I do know about women, I know that they never *voluntarily* go anywhere without their makeup. So it's a good chance Shirlene did not go of her own free will.

"Unless this guy was a professional, he had to have left some type of clue," said Billings.

"I was just thinking the opposite. Shirlene is a very clever lady. Her and Anna are always talking about strange schemes for her murder mysteries. Perhaps she left us a clue, and that's what the person who made this mess was in search of," I suggested, as I rubbed my chin in deep thought.

"Well, amateurs are always hiding their valuables in the toilet tank. I'll check." Billings added.

The captain quickly interjected, "No, that's not possible. Ships don't have tanks. All waste goes through the waste incineration system on the bottom deck."

Billings and I both sighed and kept looking. I suggested the air vents, so I checked both of them.

Another dead end.

"Does it have to be an air vent?" asked the captain.

"What do you mean?" I replied.

"Well, on ships, we have a vent-like drain on the wall of the shower where the water goes. It's right below the faucet."

Billings and I rushed over to the shower and found the vent. I used a coin to loosen the four screws and remove the grate. There was definitely something inside. I reached my hand a few inches inside and felt around. There was some type of cloth taped to the top part of the drain. I slowly peeled it back and pulled my hand out.

Billings and the Captain gathered around me. I was eager to open it, but knew there was something I had to do first.

"Uh, I don't know how to say this, Captain, but we're going to have to ask you to wait outside, sorry. This is an active investigation and we don't know what we're about to uncover here."

The captain nodded his head in acknowledgement and backed out of the cabin, mentioning some coordinates he needed to double-check before they set sail.

Billings and I headed over to a desk by the window and opened the cloth to examine it. It looks like some type of broken pendant. Perhaps even a really old and expensive pendant.

"Holy crap, sir. This case is getting stranger by the minute."

"I'll say. Grab your phone and take pictures. We need to send this to our rare gems specialist in the High Crimes Theft Task Force. He specializes in museum thefts around the world."

While we were waiting for a response, we headed to the food court inside the mall on the ship for some lunch.

Most of the vendors were not fully functional yet, so it was a toss-up between tacos and burgers. Since tacos are easier to walk and eat with, we chose those. I was chomping on a beef burrito and Billings was devouring two shrimp tempura tacos with Pico de Gallo when my phone chirped.

It was the task force specialist. His nickname was Jewels, *as one might expect*, and he was full of valuable information for us. No pun intended.

I put him on speaker. "Yeah. Go 'head, Jewels."

"Hello to you too, Solace."

"Whatcha got for us?"

Jewels sighed and continued, "Well, first off, I don't know how you two managed to get a hold of this rare piece, but kudos to you. It traces back to an artifact collection stored in a museum in England. I have a friend over there who could possibly help."

We took down the connection's name and hung up, but not before thanking him profusely. His connection was Professor Henry Davies of the University of Cambridge.

I took the lead on the call to England and placed the call on speaker. After being transferred several times, the professor answered.

"Hello."

"Yes, is this Professor Henry Davies?" I asked.

"Yes, this is he. To whom am I speaking?"

"My name is Detective John Solace and I am working on a case involving a missing woman and your name came up in the investigation."

"My name. Well, whatever do you mean? Certainly you don't think I kidnapped her! I've been in my office all day!" he laughed heartily.

Billings and I exchanged a look of confusion and I continued.

"Not at all, Professor. The woman's name is Shirlene Booker and during a search of her property, we came across an artifact. Our associate, Jewels, from the High Crimes Theft Task Force, looked at it and said you may be able to help."

"Ah, Jewels! How is the ole' chap? Still a player amongst the ladies over there in the States?"

"Jewels? Well, I wouldn't know, actually. Um. Can I send you a photo to look at?"

"Well, I most certainly know what Jewels looks like!" he bellowed.

"No, I meant the artifact. Oh wait, you were making a joke. I get it."

I wondered if the professor was 'all there'.

"Just joshing with you, my inquisitive friend. Certainly. I suppose you want to 'text message' it to my mobile like the young students often do?"

I confirmed I wanted to 'text message' it and took down his number.

After what seemed like an eternity, he finished reviewing the image and spoke, but in a faint whisper.

"This is impossible. How did you…? Why yes, I know this collection personally and also know the family who… came into its possession. But I will only speak in person. I must go now. I have a class waiting."

The call immediately disconnected, and I looked at Billings in bewilderment. Billings put both his hands up to indicate he had no idea what had just happened, either.

"What now? Do we actually believe this 'nutty professor?'" I questioned aloud.

Billings was about to answer when his phone chirped. "Well, I'll be…"

"What?"

"You won't believe this, sir, but we just got a hit on one of Shirlene's credit cards. You'll never believe where it originated from."

"Let me guess… England?"

"Yes, sir. Looks like we'll be seeing the professor in person after all."

"If the captain approves it, yeah. "

We left the ship and headed back to the airport. After a rather loud conversation with the captain about budgets and overtime, he finally okayed the expense, but with certain stipulations.

I called Anna directly after I hung up. She finally picked up.

"I can explain everything, dear. You see—" Anna said hastily.

"Anna, that's not why I'm calling. You will not believe where the case has just led us to?"

"Um, England?"

"How the heck did you–?! Ugh! Nevermind. Pack your bags. We're going on a treasure hunt."

| CHAPTER 6

Making the Connection...
Can you hear me now?

Sergio Wright

I turned right onto the long driveway and took in the scenery: tall trees that seem to crowd together to cover me from the open sky and the smell of salt air from the water that surrounded the property. I arrived at the meeting spot and parked. As I entered, I found Ernest by the gate that led to the lower level. As usual, he had on a snazzy outfit with his wavy hair slicked back, a gray Trilby hat tilted to the side, and that stupid smirk on his face.

"Hey, boss! How's it goin'? The 'package' is all locked up. The morphine is probably just wearing off."

Though he was imprisoned in England, Ernest the conman was originally from New York. I hated that wise-guy accent and couldn't wait to be done with this man for good.

"Nevermind that. Do you have the relic?"

"Unfortunately, my contact could not find it. I mean, he tore the room apart, I swear. And then, before he could finish, the cops showed up and he had to bolt!"

"You moron! I warned you what would happen if you messed up again! You can forget about that final installment to your account! Be grateful I'm letting off with your life. Now give me the key and get out of my sight!"

Ernest hands him the key, points towards the lower level, and shakes his head.

He looks at Sergio and says, "It's been real, Mr. Wright", and tips his hat.

"Wait!"

"Yeah."

"Be sure to lie low for a while. The cops are still looking for her and they could soon be looking for you, too."

"Nah. We covered our tracks too good. They're not traveling to England to look for no broad. I don't care how important she is," Ernest chuckled as he left the building.

I hope not. But right now, I needed a new plan, and I think I knew just what to do. My illegitimate bastard sister was going to tell me what I needed to know. Or else.

Before going downstairs, I head to the control room to check her out first. I found the monitor that was zoomed in on her and moved in close to examine her. She was coming to and was probably confused about the stone floors and murals on the walls. Thinking about my mother, I wondered what she would have thought about my plan. I was contemplating harming a child that she had conceived and who I'm sure she loved. I moved back from the screen and sat down in the rolling office chair to think. I stared at this woman for hours through the monitor, seeing if there was any resemblance to me. Maybe the nose and the shape of the eyes, but who cares? She was trying to take what was rightfully mine, and she means nothing to me!

This so-called sister never gave a damn about me or even tried to find me. I remember when I turned twenty-two, and they told me what my father had left me to inherit. I was in shock at the collection of jewels and artifacts that were to be mine. But none of the other relics were worth even a fraction of the Tristan's Corinthian Cross. However, the relic only retained its value if both pieces were locked together to uncover the hidden ruby in the center. And, Father had given it to this woman? For what? No one ever even spoke of her growing up, like she never existed. And, in my mind, she didn't.

I stood up, walked back to the gate, and pulled out the key. It was time I confronted this woman once and for all.

As I descended the staircase, I thought about how to place the blame on Ernest for whatever 'justice' shall come to this 'missing' woman, who won't be missing for long.

I walked into the room and faced the thief who had stolen everything from me.

She sat up and looked at me with a perplexed look on her face, asking questions like, "Who are you? Where am I? What's going on?"

"As if you don't know. I should have known you'd play dumb. Where is the relic? Answer me! Or, you'll be sorry!"

My fury had taken over. I never could have prepared myself for what happened next.

CHAPTER 7

My Evil Twin

Shirlene

My head was killing me, like I had been given something to knock me out. I remember vaguely being on a plane with Ernest and him telling me he was a con man who only pretended to be wealthy and interested in me because he was hired to do so. I should have known it was too good to be true. But why kidnap me and bring me here? Wherever here is?

It looked like a museum with marble floors and elaborate murals on the walls and ceiling, minus the line of bars preventing me from leaving. Men and women of the 16th century stared at me in various positions, some clothed and some not. The murals reminded me of the Michaelangelo Renaissance era. While I was staring at one scene called the Tempest, signed by Giorgione, items on the floor caught the corner caught my eye. It was a sandwich and bottled water. It was the least Ernest could do, I suppose, after deceiving me. How would I ever explain all of this to Anna? If I ever made it home alive? Hopefully, Anna has John looking for me.

I was about to reach for the water bottle when the steel bars rose behind me. A distinguished-looking man walked in glaring at me with deep-set eyes kind of similar to mine. He wore a tailored black shirt with black pants and a long wool coat with a scarf and leather gloves. The heels of his shoes clicked toward me slowly. He stopped in front of me and stared, not saying a word.

I couldn't stand the silence, so I spoke first. "Where am I? Why did you pay Ernest to trick me and bring me here? What do you want with me?"

The mysterious man finally spoke. "Ms. Shirlene Booker. The mastermind behind this whole heist. I never thought my father would fall for your pathetic act. What did you do? Call him up while he was ill, crying, asking him to change his will?"

"What act? What are you talking about?" I pleaded. "I just want to go home."

"Please. Just stop. Your little innocent act won't work on me… sis."

The reality of the situation became very real, and suddenly, fear took over my body. I took a sip of water to compose myself, but I could barely speak. "I.. I … don't know what you're talking about, mister, but I am not your sister. I was an only child my entire life. And, and not only that, my adoptive parents had no kids of their own. I swear it."

Once again, he stared at me, baffled, for what seemed to be ages, and eventually, tilted his head and opened his mouth slightly as if he had solved a case.

"You really don't know, do you?"

"No. That's what I've been trying to tell you!" I urged.

The man immediately shot up straight, held his head up high, and returned to his stoic state.

"Well, I don't care if you know the story or not. You better hand over the relic or your measly life will be over! Do you understand?!"

I thought about everything he was saying and everything that had transpired since I met Ernest. Several weeks ago, I had received a mysterious package from England. The message only read, "I hope you had a good life. We are sorry. Cherish this forever and you will find your other half that makes the ruby shine bright, my dear Shirlene."

I hadn't an inkling what any of it meant. And suddenly, I was feeling woozy. Now this man is saying I'm his sister. "Please, I… I need to know the story. Then I'll tell you what you want to know."

He told me his name was Sergio Wright, son of Sir Ricardo Wright and Isabella. Sergio grew up in a castle and was the rightful heir to the family treasures. Then, with the most callous tone, the story continued of the child born out of wedlock, *which was supposedly me*, who was sent away to the States after birth. The mother had always longed for a little girl, but the father felt he could not raise another man's child. And, if people found out about his wife's indiscretions, his reputation would be ruined. But, in the end, it seems Ricardo Wright felt regret and shame for turning away the child. Me.

It was apparent Sergio was angry. Angry at his parents, angry at me, angry at the world. It was a treasure he felt he had earned. But obviously, his father wanted both of us to have it for a reason. Perhaps to bring us together as a family? We're both alone in this world. Maybe he wanted us to have each other.

Sergio, my half brother, had finished his story. I looked up at him and said, "Your father sent it to me weeks ago. I brought it with me on the ship and hid it in the shower drain. I hope it brings you some kind of peace. I never asked for any of this."

I was hoping by telling Sergio what he wanted, it would save my life. Honestly, the look in his eyes was so evil, I feared what he might do to me if I resisted. I just wanted to go home, back to my normal life, being just another Booker, a book publicist for authors. A nobody.

As soon as I finished telling him what he demanded, he pulled his cell phone out and started dialing. I could hear him yelling at Ernest to tell his contact to check the shower drain, but was cut short by Ernest and it seems, more bad news. The police had seized something from the room and left the ship. After cursing into the phone, he disconnected and charged toward me.

He grabbed me and lifted me off the floor by my shirt collar, screamed it was all my fault, and threw me back down onto the cold, hard marble floor.

"You're no family of mine! You *never* were, and *never* will be!"

I cowered in the corner and sobbed uncontrollably as the metal bars of the gate lowered and I was trapped once again.

CHAPTER 8 |

A History Lesson in Wright and Wrong

John

I couldn't believe I was on a plane flying to England with rosebud. As we touched down, the view of the countryside, castles, and greenery was amazing. Everyone could not help but point and gasp during the entire descent. Everyone, including Putnam. I guess Billings was trying to make the trip a 'couples' thing. I could tell from their body language things were a bit tense between them.

The trip was costing us a pretty penny, since the department only okayed (and paid for) the trip for me and Billings. And, both of us had enough vacation time saved up for three two-week vacations, so the department couldn't really refuse. Plus, if we solve this case, it could mean a lot of positive press coverage for the entire precinct.

"Isn't this incredible John?" Anna said.

"I've never seen anything like it." I responded. Although, I was referring to the view outside the window and my rosebud. She was all dolled up in a red rose-patterned sweater, black skirt, and boots. And dangling from her ears were the red rose earrings I bought her last Christmas. We exited the plane and followed signs for the rental car counter. While the others visited the restrooms and grabbed our luggage from the rotating machines, I headed for the counter to claim our car reservation. I was clutching the jewel case tightly, as I had been the entire trip. Holding something that could be worth millions will do that to an average, blue-collar person like me. The case was a small black safe that was not only fire and waterproof but also included biometric features. Both Billings and I would need to use the scanner to open it.

"Reservation for Solace, John Solace."

"Of course, you reserved the SUV, correct?"

I nodded as confirmation. The blonde-haired woman in the crisply starched uniform and bun at the nape of her neck spoke with a lovely accent that made even the contract legalese she was reciting sound interesting. I nodded again as if I understood and signed on the dotted line. A few minutes later, I was holding the keys and went in search of the others.

Billings found me first. "All set with the car, boss?"

"Yep. I hope you have your map handy, because I am clueless about where we are going."

"Did I hear you correctly, dear? Are you admitting to being lost before we even get on the road?" Anna approached, chuckling at her own joke, while Putnam joined in. I could tell she was trying to hide her mounting fears about finding Shirlene.

"Yeah, yeah, yeah, laugh it up. We are in another country, you know? I'm allowed to be confused."

"I'd be happy to drive, boss! I visited here once, ages ago." Billings said with his hand open for the keys.

I tossed them over with a shrug. "Fine by me."

We were traveling to the University of Cambridge to see Professor Henry Davies. I did some research on my phone while Billings drove. The university was granted a royal charter by Henry III in 1231, and is the second-oldest university in the English-speaking world and the world's fourth-oldest surviving university. It is also renowned as one of the most prestigious academic institutions in the world. They built most of the city on the east bank of the River Cam and off The Fen Causeway.

I paused from my light internet research to look out the window at the view. I was amazed Anna was not snapping pictures, but I understood why she wasn't. While the country was stunning, we had one primary goal for being here, and that was to find Shirlene. This was also the first time she had left her babies alone for a long period of time, intentionally, that is. Although she has called Bonnie five times already since we left to update her 'cat-sitting' instructions. When I think back to the kidnapping case where we first met, I cannot believe it will be two years in a month. I remember that first night I spent in her living room combing through her novels, trying to find a clue to her whereabouts, meeting her babies for the first time, and caring for them until she returned home. Now, they are a part of my family too, especially Tiny.

I was jarred from my thoughts by Putnam in the front seat. She was adamantly explaining to Billings the police procedures in England and how the U.S. could learn a thing or two about respect and formalities. Barely listening, Billings concentrated on the overly narrow streets and getting used to driving on the opposite side of the road, and inserted a polite 'uh-huh' every few minutes.

We pulled onto the university grounds in under an hour. Seven hundred acres of history. There were magnificent structures with towering steeples everywhere. Anna pointed to a chapel with beautiful stained-glass windows and we all took in the sight.

Using the campus directory and map online, we were able to locate Pembroke St., and eventually, parked off of Downing St. and walked to the Museum of Archaeology and Anthropology. Upon entering the building, we could see all the relics from the past on display in glass cases and other secure devices. The museum was closed today, so we were the only people in the building. Our voices echoed from the twenty-foot vaulted ceilings down the seemingly never-ending corridors.

Professor Davies stepped into the lobby from a back corridor to greet us. He was a small man with a frazzled look and the hair to match. His thick mustache and eyebrows seem to complement the look. He wore a brown tweed suit with a matching vest and a collared shirt I'm sure had, at some point, been white.

"Welcome, gentlemen and ladies, to England. And to the University of Cambridge, of course. Come, come, this way, to my workspace in the back." He gestured quickly and shuffled along the linoleum floors at a pace that seemed faster than his feet could handle.

We all slowed our pace to match his, so as not to pass him. Eventually, we entered a room that was full of display cases with relics, a workstation with a magnifier desk lamp, trowels, and what he explained were scanning electron microscopes. However, most of the room's surfaces were covered in papers, files, and books.

Professor Davies didn't even bother apologizing for the mess. He just moved the clutter from the two chairs to the desk and gestured for us to sit. Billings and I let the girls sit while we turned towards the professor and got right to the point.

"So, professor, what can you tell us about the relic?" I ventured.

"First things first. May I see it?" he countered. "I have to be sure my initial assessment is indeed correct."

"Oh, of course," I replied. I set down the box and entered the secure code. Next, Billings and I placed our fingers on the biometric scanner and the box opened. Professor Davies handed me a pair of latex gloves and donned a pair himself.

I handed him the relic, that was wrapped in a protective cloth.

The professor pulls uses his magnifier desk lamp and quietly examines it while muttering a series of 'hmmm's', 'aha's', and 'interesting's'.

Eventually, he looked up and declared, "This relic is not 'broken', as you said on the phone. Furthermore, this is not related to the relic stored at the National History Museum in England. It is just as I suspected. The Tristan's Corinthian Cross, part of a collection acquired by the Wright Foundation thirty years ago, which was run by Ricardo Wright."

As if deep in thought, he turned away and continued on. "I remember when the relics were first found during an excavation in 1954. It was referred to as the Hoffshire Hoard and contained some of the rarest of Anglo-Saxon gold. Archaeologists have determined it is likely art thieves from the kingdoms of Northumbria and Wessex seized the treasures. Rumor has it Ricardo Wright's son, Sergio, stands to inherit it all."

Billings jumped in, trying not to sound impatient, "So, if it's not broken, then why does it look like that?"

"Ahhh, good question. It is part of a puzzle which can only be solved if the matching piece is found. Masterfully designed to 'function' when the two parts are connected. I had only heard of such myths, but never saw one up close. See the hollow ridges?" he said in a hushed voice. "Those ridges allow the relics to interlock like a puzzle piece."

"And then what? What happens then?" Anna interjected curiously. Up to this point, she had been rather quiet.

"Magic, my dear Watson! As our friend, Jewels, would say!" throwing his hands up in the air with excitement.

"When the pieces interlock, it is said that the rarest of rubies is revealed, and the Hoffshire collection is complete. This would make Sergio the wealthiest man in the country."

"I just don't understand the connection, John," Anna gushed frantically. "What does any of this have to do with Shirlene? Even if this Sergio is looking for this missing piece, how did she even get it? She has <u>nothing</u> to do with <u>any</u> of this!"

"Relax, dear. Let's just think for a minute. Did she ever mention family in England?"

"No. Her family was from Rhode Island."

"What about the mysterious man? Is he from England?"

"Not that she mentioned, no. But, as I told you before we left, she was googling a lot of strange things about relics in England on her tablet."

Putnam and Billings interrupted and tried to further pacify Anna's worries. "Don't worry Anna, we're going to figure all this out <u>together</u> and find Shirlene." Putnam took Anna's hand and squeezed it once as a sign of support.

"We need to find this Sergio, and see what he knows. He <u>has to</u> be the key to finding Shirlene." I concluded.

A moment later, Professor Davies was shuffling us back out to the lobby. "Please let me know if you find the missing piece and if you need any more information. Always happy to help the bobbies!" He waved us out of the building hurriedly, even as we thanked him generously.

Putnam was explaining to us how police officers were called 'bobbies' and 'peelers' in England, when the professor sprang out of the door, calling us back urgently.

"Detective Solace! One more thing!" the professor called out from the door.

"What's that, Professor?"

"Be very careful. I must warn you of the immense power the Wright family has over everything in England, from the government to the constabulary officials. Good luck to you all!"

I replied, "Thanks, Professor," thinking to myself 'good luck' would have sufficed. His ominous words were a warning all of us contemplated as we strode back to the car.

Billings looked at me as if reading my thoughts. "Are you thinking what I'm thinking, boss?"

"Yep. We need resources. Local resources."

"Exactly. Next stop, the Cambridgeshire Constabulary!"

Halfway to our destination, we spotted a pub and stopped to recharge. It was obvious we would not make it to the hotel any time soon. In the end, we all decided on fish and chips and devoured it like we hadn't eaten for days.

Once we arrived at the Constabulary, I could feel it in my bones. We were one step closer to solving this mystery.

"Welcome to Cambridgeshire Constabulary, Detectives… and ladies, of course!" the man in a simple dress shirt, tie, and slacks declared. He was standing next to the front desk of the lobby, where a man in uniform, including the tall helmet with his badge on it, smiled awkwardly.

We all thanked him and shook his hand.

"I'm Chief Inspector Taylor and this is Constable Fernsby. I've already been briefed by your captain and have a room waiting for you. Right this way."

"Thank you, sir," Billings and I uttered almost simultaneously.

The white board was already set up in the conference room. Pictures of Shirlene and the relic had been added. We filled in CI Taylor on what we learned from the professor and told him about his warning. Soon after, images of the Wright family graced the board. Now it was time to connect the dots.

Constable Fernsby stepped into the doorway to listen in. CI Taylor invited him to join us and provide some insight.

"Constable Fernsby has lived here his whole life and knows all about the Wright family. I'll let him fill you in."

"Yes, sir, of course. Well, the professor's warning was not all untrue. They control much of the property, businesses, and organizations all over England, and they are a very prestigious family with various homes, including their main castle about fifty miles down the road."

"Great, let's just go to the castle and talk to this Sergio guy!" Putnam blurted out. Apparently, as agitated as the rest of us.

"I'm afraid that's not possible, ma'am," Constable Fernsby responded. "Sergio hasn't been seen for years. And, it's said that only the maintenance staff and groundskeepers attend to the home during the week."

"Ugh! This case is infuriating," Anna bellowed.

I was already on the computer set up on the conference table doing a 'deep dive" into living relatives of the Wright family. "Hey, it says here, the sister of Ricardo Wright's wife, Isabella, is the only living relative. She lives at some assisted living facility in Over. Where's that? Is it far from here?"

"Not far. It's a large village near the *River Great Ouse* right here in Cambridgeshire. I can direct you," Constable Fernsby clarified.

"And I can call ahead and make sure that *before* you arrive, you have the access you need to speak to her," offered CI Taylor. "And Constable Fernsby will get you set up with a travel laptop, just in case."

"Much appreciated, sir."

We left the Cambridgeshire Constabulary with a feeling of purpose. But I had to wonder how many layers of this puzzle there would be before we found Shirlene. I could see the same concern on Anna's face, so I put my arm around her and pulled her close as we retreated to the car once more.

We all buckled our seatbelts and prepared for the short ride to Over, where Rayna Wright awaited.

CHAPTER 9

Shining Lights and Vacations in Maine

Anna

Under different circumstances, I would beg John to go sightseeing, but all I could think about was my friend. I still do not know what any of this relic business has to do with Shirlene, and this Sergio guy sounds awfully dangerous. In fact, this whole family sounds dangerous, with their money, jewels, and power. I just hope this lead can tell us more.

Eventually, we reached the town of Over, where their attempt to expand with modern housing and commercial structures clashed with the historic structures that remained. My research on Wikipedia indicated the oldest remaining structure in Over is now believed to be from the wall running down Fen End to the Willingham Road corner, standing for over 500 years.

Finally, we reached the assisted living facility. The sign that greeted us was mostly covered in shrubbery, so I could only make out Over Yonder. The road that led to the main complex was shaded, as the trees high above on either side of the road joined like interlocking hands. Maybe they were protecting us?

A woman in a white nursing uniform met us in the parking lot. She had her arms folded in front of her chest and was looking down at her watch as if annoyed. As we exited the car and approached her, she looked down at us over her thin wireframe glasses.

John and Billings went ahead, and John reached out to shake her hand as he introduced everyone. She simply looked up and said, "You're late. This way."

We all followed in silence as she led the way through security, gave us all visitor badges to clip on our shirts, and passed through several secure doors before we reached the 'Main Rec Room', based on the sign.

After some whispering between them, another nurse took over the 'tour', extended her arm, and led us out to the balcony area.

She turned to us and said, "Miss Rayna is right over there. But I must warn you, more often than not, she is barely lucid, so you can't believe everything she says. She's in the late stages of dementia."

"Does her nephew, Sergio, visit often?" I asked.

"No, I did not realize she had any living family members," she replied. As she turned to go back inside, she pointed to the doorway and let us know she was right there if we needed her.

I turned back to look at the frail woman in the wheelchair. She had long gray hair styled in a French braid, a face etched with lines that told the stories of her life, and a checkered blanket laid across her legs. For a moment, I thought of my mother; but before the guilt of not calling or visiting her enough washed over me, I snapped out of it. I noticed that while the rest of the woman's body seemed hunched over and defeated, like she had given up on life, her green eyes were surprisingly alert. She smiled as we approached her.

John introduced himself while Billings and Putnam stood back, not wanting to overwhelm her. John started with questions about her sister's husband and asked if she remembered when he purchased the collection.

Clearly troubled by the line of questions, Rayna's smile disappeared and her eyes went dark. She began shaking her head back and forth frantically. I rushed over, interjected, and tried to calm her down.

"It's okay, Rayna, tell me what's wrong? What are you afraid of, dear?"

She continued shaking her head back and forth and began a chant of some sort. "Shhh, shhh, a promise is a promise. Shhh, shhh, a promise is a promise."

"What promise? What did you promise, Rayna?" John and I both inquired in unison.

"A promise is a promise. You don't disclose the family secret. EVER!"

I leaned in and whispered, "Rayna, it's okay, dear. Isabella would approve if you told this one time. Another woman's life is in danger. A woman I care about deeply. Do you understand?"

Rayna stopped rocking. She turned to me and stared into my eyes. They had gotten even darker and colder than before. She raised her hand slowly, put it up to my ear as children do when they are telling a secret they don't want anyone to hear, and whispered, "It's a horrible story of the bastard child. Sent away 'cause no one wanted her."

My face went white. Was she lucid right now? What if Shirlene was the child? Is that possible? I stepped away to the far corner of the balcony and relayed what Rayna had said.

Putnam whispered loudly, "Oh my goodness, that would make Sergio her brother!"

Billings chimed in, "Yeah, and it would also make him furious if he now has to share his inheritance!"

"Agreed. Do you want me to ask her about Sergio?" I asked John.

"Yeah, let's give it a try. You seem to have a rapport with her."

I hurried back to Rayna's side and asked if she knew where Sergio was.

"He was such a quiet and curious child. Always playing hide and seek with Isabella."

Trying to keep her talking, I said, "Oh, okay. Sounds like he had lots of fun with his mother."

"Oh yes, unless he was in trouble. Then you would never find him for hours. Isabella was quite concerned for the boy."

"Oh my. I could understand why. Did Sergio have a favorite place he would go when he was in trouble?"

Rayna began rocking again, and then escalated to pointing and shouting, "It was right on the water, so tall! It shined so bright! Can you see it?"

Now attracting more attention than we would have liked, the nurse rushed in and cut the interview short, saying Rayna needed to rest.

Another annoyed nurse angrily showed us out and collected our badges.

As we dashed to the car, I wondered about the connection to Shirlene and if we were any closer to finding her. I'm sure everyone was thinking the same thing. What was right on the water, very tall, and shined bright?

It was Putnam who spoke first. "I think I've got it! I just need to look at the map again."

Opening the car to grab the map and sprawling it out on the hood, she continued, "I remember looking at the Wright family's list of properties on the map earlier. There's a house right on the water and you know what else is there?"

We all guessed incorrectly, calling out answers such as boats, docks, and the like.

Putnam shook her head, "No, no. I remember from my family vacations in Maine—lighthouses!"

It was an 'aha' moment for all of us.

Putnam gave Billings the address to the Wright lighthouse property, and we were off.

227 Brighthouse Lane, here we come!

CHAPTER 10 |

A Major Cliffhanger with a Side of Smelling Salts

John

Boy, was I surprised by how well Anna handled Rayna. So calm and reassuring. We would have never gotten that much information without her.

And Billings was getting to be a pro at navigating the roads in England. Even though he'd been here ages ago, it all came back to him rather instinctively.

It was late evening by the time we arrived, and the property was dark and desolate. Small spotlights thrust deep into the grass illuminated the driveway on either side and seemed to increase the eeriness of the night. I did not know what we were going to find and was glad the laptop CI Taylor had given us had a location tracker device. Just in case, I texted him our findings and where we headed.

As we came around the bin, the enormous structure came into view. I wonder how this compared to their main castle. The property had to be <u>at least</u> 8,000 square feet.

Nestled behind the castle was the grand lighthouse, towering high above it, on the edge of the cliff overlooking the water. It was breathtaking and I could stare it out all night, but I had a crime to solve and Anna was counting on me to find Shirlene.

We all got out and grabbed the supplies we would need to investigate at night. I handed Anna a flashlight. "Come on, let's check the doors of this… castle." I said. "I got the front. Billings, Putnam, check around the side and rear."

I took Anna's hand and told her to stay close. There were two doors in the front and neither would budge, so we met Billings and Putnam around the back.

"Any luck?" I asked.

"No luck, sir," Billings responded.

"Well, I guess it's time to check out the 'tall light on the water, that shines so bright'," I said.

We made our way behind the property towards the lighthouse. Luckily, there was a small footpath to guide the way. As the lighthouse came into view, so did the edge of the cliff and the roaring waves splashing up on the rocks and leaping towards us. We all leaped back in unison and commented on the need for a safety banister along the footpath to prevent visitors from going over the cliff and into the waters.

Putnam was the first to reach the entrance of the lighthouse; grimacing as she pulled open the heavy iron doors. It seemed odd that the castle was locked up tight, but not the lighthouse.

"Hold on, Putnam. You check around the perimeter with Anna. Stick together, alright?" I turned to Billings. "Let's secure the inside and make sure there are no *surprises* waiting."

"I agree, sir. This place at night is a bit creepy, if you ask me."

The inside of the main lobby was all white stone. There seemed to be three levels: the main level, the upper level, and the lower level. When we gazed up past the steep, narrow spiral staircase, what was visible was an abyss of darkness. Billings seemed uneasy, *and honestly, so was I*, so I decided we should investigate the lower level first. Lights in the floor led us down a wider spiral staircase, but we still used our flashlights. As we approached the last step and looked up, we were shocked by the murals everywhere. Just another majestic beauty of England. If only we were here under different circumstances.

Planes, Trains, and Relics of the Past

We turned toward the back area, which seemed to be a gated storage space. Billings used his flashlight to find the panel with a switch. After busting the panel open, he flipped it on. The gate rose slowly and there was Shirlene — sprawled on the floor in the corner!

"Shirlene! Shirlene! Can you hear me?" I shouted.

Billings was on the phone summoning Putnam and telling her to contact CI Taylor right away.

"Hang on Shirlene! Help is on the way!"

I tried CPR to resuscitate her, but it was not working. Billings and I were worried she had been drugged.

Suddenly, I was transported back to the moment I saw Doc Bernstein wheeling my brother out of the LOV building in a body bag. Time seemed to freeze for a second and my breathing had quickened as a wave of emotions rushed over me as I stared at Shirlene's lifeless body. At that very moment, a loud voice echoed through the room. It was coming from the speaker in the far corner.

"Don't worry detective, she's not dead. Just slightly drugged, dehydrated, and exhausted. I give you credit for excellent police work, sir."

The person was clapping extra slowly and mockingly as he spoke into the microphone.

I realized who the voice could belong to. I said, "Is that you, Sergio? It's over, just give yourself up. Leave your sister out of this!"

I must have angered him because there was a loud crack followed by a screeching sound, like feedback, coming from the speaker. Billings and I held our ears. He finally spoke again. "Shirlene Booker is NO SISTER OF MINE! Mother did not want her; in fact, NO ONE WANTED HER. Stupid old man thought he could buy her forgiveness by splitting the last relic in the collection! The inheritance is MINE and I'm NOT SPLITTING IT WITH <u>ANYONE</u>!"

It was all coming together now. Perhaps not why the relic was sent to Shirlene in the first place, but why she became a threat to Sergio. I'm assuming Sergio is responsible for her new 'love interest' as well. It was all part of his plan to get rid of her.

Shirlene did not know she was even a part of this family. And I'm sure she didn't want any inheritance if it wound up costing her her life.

The mic squawked, and it got quiet. "Sergio, are you there? Hello?"

Just then, I heard a series of voices coming from upstairs calling for me and Billings. We assumed it was the paramedics and police and both yelled, "Down here!"

They found us behind the gate kneeling over Shirlene, and rushed over to get to work, trying to determine if CPR should be continued.

Constable Fernsby and CI Taylor weren't far behind.

"Well, it seems you solved the mystery case and found your friend, Detective. Congratulations. Will she be okay?" CI Taylor asked.

One paramedic jumped in and replied, "She's fine. The smelling salts are working. Probably just passed out from stress, exhaustion, and dehydration. We'll be sure to have the hospital run a toxicology screening, just to be safe."

We all gave a sigh of relief.

I turned to CI Taylor and gave him the somber update. "We have a problem, sir. Sergio was here, talking to us through the PA system. This whole thing was about the relic. Apparently, he is furious with his father. Perhaps he was the one who sent the other half of the relic to Shirlene. Sergio needed the entire relic to complete the collection and gain the true value of his inheritance. We have to find him! Shirlene could still be in danger."

Billings responded, "But he could have been speaking through the system from anywhere. For all we know, he is miles away and not even on the grounds, sir."

I nodded in agreement and Constable Fernsby suggested we check the upper floors anyway.

The paramedics had Shirlene, and we were all headed towards the staircase when Putnam and Anna rushed in.

"Shirlene! It's me, Anna! Oh my gosh, I'm so glad you're okay!" she said as she hugged her awkwardly, not sure if she was hurt anywhere.

Shirlene mumbled softly, but it was incoherent.

"She's going to be okay, right?" Anna asked the paramedics.

They assured her she was and moved her to the ambulance. Anna insisted on riding with her.

"Putnam, can you follow the ambulance to the hospital and stay with Anna? We're going to try and find Sergio."

"Of course, you think he's here?"

"No idea, but we're going to search the grounds inside and out."

After they left, we all turned back towards the lighthouse. CI Taylor and his team of constables, awaiting direction outside, huddled briefly to determine their game plan. Half of them would search the grounds and the others would head to the lighthouse. Billings and I were up front with CI Taylor and the first to ascend the dark spiral staircase with our flashlights out.

At the top of the stairs, there was just one room with the doors flung open. It was an empty control room on the top floor with at least six video monitors recording various locations within the lighthouse and a mic at the helm where I assumed he was speaking to us from. However, the room was empty. He must have had an escape route already planned, but besides the staircase, it wasn't obvious to us. Just a small circular window and what looked like a storage closet in the corner.

Constable Fernsby walked over to further inspect the small closet. As he moved boxes to the side, a silver door came into view. It was apparent what we were looking at was an elevator.

"I had a feeling there was a secret entrance. I remember reading about it online. They were built into many of the rooms in their homes as well, sir," Fernsby explained.

"I'm assuming it leads to an exit outside?" I added.

"Only one way to find out," said Billings. "I'll meet you all downstairs, if that's okay, sir."

"Have fun. See you downstairs."

We all exited to the rear of the property where we thought Billings would end up. And, sure enough, there he was, pushing open a stone doorway that blended with the building exterior so it was invisible to the naked eye.

"Well, how 'bout that! We know how he escaped, but the trick is to figure out where he went. Someone like him has enough money to disappear forever," I declared.

"Listen, Detective, why don't you let me and my men handle it from here? You and your partner should head over to the hospital to be with your friends."

I asked if he was sure and he promised us he would keep us posted on the investigation, even after we went back to the States. There were charges of kidnapping, fraud, and assault, at the very least, in store for Sergio Wright.

After returning his laptop, we waved 'so long' from the car and headed to Milton Keynes University Hospital to meet up with the girls.

CHAPTER 11 |

Ditching Online Dating for London

Anna

I had been here most of the night on something resembling a couch along the opposite side of the room and the sun was just peeking its head up over the horizon, as if playing a game of hide and seek… checking to see if the 'seeker' was close by.

Shirlene had either been asleep or wheeled away for some type of test most of the time, so I hadn't had the chance to really speak to her. And Putnam left a constable outside the room while she went to the hotel to shower and rest a few hours.

Listening to the beep on the heart machine reminded me of when I was in the hospital after the boat explosion. I also recalled the soothing, yet slightly agitating, southern drawl of the nurse who took care of me. Although some would call her 'bubbly' and 'perky', other words come to mind when you are experiencing it every hour on the hour, all throughout the night. Ha!

Shirlene's nurse was the exact opposite.

"Rise and shine, toots!" a voice bellowed from the doorway. Shirlene slowly opened her eyes, but quickly covered them from the crack of light coming from the slit in the curtains.

The voice also startled me from my thoughts. It was coming from Nurse Harlee. A busty woman with short, curly hair, a sizable mole on her nose, broad shoulders, and a voice like my Uncle Leo, on my dad's side of the family, a true bass in the church choir.

She was wheeling in a cart with syringes and tubes.

"It's bloodwork time! Give us a minute, will ya?" she asked, in what I assumed was her most polite voice.

I nodded and went out into the hallway to follow the blue arrow to the elevator, where the coffee machine was tucked away in a blue room off to the right. I was standing behind a gentleman who was fighting with the machine to take his overly wrinkled dollar bill when the elevators opened. John and Billings rushed into the corridor, pointing to the arrow on the floor and talking in a loud whisper. They couldn't see me from the hidden blue room, but I saw them.

"John!"

"Anna! How are you? How's Shirlene? Still stable?"

"Yes, thank God. I cannot imagine how scared she must've been."

"And confused," said Billings.

"Yeah, that too," I replied.

"Well, I'd like to talk to her and get her statement, if possible," asked John, as he grabbed my hand to guide me down the hallway.

"Okay. If you must. But first, coffee."

* * *

Nurse Haylee was just leaving when we approached the room. I nodded while John and Billings made pleasantries. She looked both of them up and down, gave a brief 'hmph', and went back to the nurse's station down the hall.

"What was that about?" Billings inquired.

"No idea," I said, shaking my head.

John entered the room first. "There's my favorite publicist. How are you feeling?"

Shirlene turned and smiled. "Flattery will get you nowhere, Detective."

Planes, Trains, and Relics of the Past

We all smiled and laughed, elated to hear Shirlene's banter—surely a sign she was on the mend.

"We're so glad you're okay. You gave us quite a scare. If you're feeling up to it, I'd like to get a statement."

Shirlene told us all to pull up a chair and began her story. It all started in her home, in Freehold, from her laptop. She was working remotely one day and an email notification popped up on her screen for an invitation to a new dating site called 'Match Made in Heaven'.

She thought it was odd, but figured one of her colleagues referred her and completed the registration process.

That was where she met Ernesto. He was the perfect gentleman and doted on her hand and foot and lavisher her with gifts. So, when he wanted her to join him on the cruise, she took a chance and sailed away with him. It had been ages since her last vacation, and she was eager to continue their budding romance on the open seas.

It wasn't until the last day on the ship that things took a turn for the worse. He started asking questions about her family, and if she had received anything special from them lately. That's when she knew she was in trouble and hid the relic in the shower drain. Soon after was when he forced her off the ship at gunpoint, shoved into a car, and apparently drugged her. While on the plane she began coming to, and remembered thinking it was strange they were the only two people on board. The next time she awoke, she overheard Ernesto on the phone telling someone that he 'had no choice but to bring her, because she won't tell me where it is'.

It was clear from her recount of the story; she was drugged and transported to the lighthouse where we found her. It was then that she learned the complete story from Sergio.

Shirlene vowed she would never try online dating again, and that she was through with men for good.

We all chuckled, and I squeezed Shirlene's hand and smiled at my friend, grateful for the bond we had.

"What's all the hoopla in here? Geez."

It was Nurse Harlee again, with some paperwork for Shirlene.

"You're all set. No concussion, your bloodwork is fine, and you're all hydrated. Whatever they gave you is gone from your system. Follow the post hospital instructions on the discharge papers and call your primary in the States with questions."

Before she turned on her heels, Shirlene thanked her, and wondered if she could ask her one last question.

We all shook our heads 'no' with wide eyes, even as Shirlene was forming the question with her mouth.

"That's an unusual name. Where does it originate from?"

I was sipping my coffee and almost choked.

"Well, isn't it obvious? I was conceived on a 1958 Harley Davidson Duo-Glide! Known for its adjustable suspension!" she roared.

We all looked at each other with wide eyes, unsure of how to respond.

Hoping to get over the awkward silence in the room, we began planning for Shirlene's discharge. Since her clothing was taken to analysis by the Crime Lab, I got her some items from the gift shop.

As I was removing the price tags for Shirlene, I thought to myself that there were actually two days left in our 'trip'. I turned to John in that moment, and said, "You know, John,

I read online that Cambridge has good rail and road access to London."

"That sounds like a great idea, sir. I mean, we do have two more days left in our 'vacation'," Billings added.

"What's a great idea?" Putnam asked as she strolled into the room freshly showered and dressed, holding a coffee cup.

Putnam and Billings embraced as he said, "We're going to London, honey!"

I confirmed with Shirlene she was up for the adventure and she was 'all in'. We all headed back to the hotel to shower and change. John used the time to check in on the case and learned Sergio was still on the run.

We had planned a day of sightseeing in the city of London, from Buckingham Palace to lunch in the Cotswolds, but we all voted to pass on the London Dinner Cruise on the Thames River, for obvious reasons. Ha!

We'd been back in the U.S. for a week now and we were having a small dinner at the house with Shirlene and Bonnie. It was a celebration of Shirlene's recovery and return, and a thank you to Bonnie for watching my babies while we were away.

I whipped up a simple dish of linguini and clams. I spiced my recipe up with clam juice, a dash of cream, and a squeeze of lemon at the end. For my dry wine, I used a good bottle of Sauvignon Blanc.

We were telling Bonnie all about the sites in London, when Shirlene brought up what she calls John and I's 'disappearing act' for almost two hours while everyone was inside Madame Tussaud's London. John and I shook our heads in denial and pleaded the fifth.

Bonnie chimed in that it did sound suspicious and pressed for answers, but I just changed the subject to dessert, Chocolate Torrone. Even though it was not Christmas, who could resist chocolate and hazelnuts? My plan worked, and the conversation shifted to chocolate.

I cleared the dinner plates and went to get a dessert dish from the kitchen while John took a work call.

He returned to the table just as I was serving the last plate.

"Everything okay, dear?" I asked.

"Yeah, that was CI Taylor with an update."

Everyone was all ears. Even Tiny's ears perked up as he crossed John's feet.

It seems they caught Ernesto in Italy somewhere, but Sergio was still on the run and Cambridgeshire Constabulary was still on the case. Such a dilemma Sergio must be in. Even if he wanted to cash in on his full inheritance, it wouldn't be worth as much without the other half of the relic. And for now, his assets had been frozen by the police. I learned a long time ago during research for a book that it's a tactic often used by law enforcement to force fugitives out of hiding. But this was not your ordinary fugitive. This one had connections all over the world. It was one perk of his father's wealth. No telling what powerful people in high places owed his father 'favors'.

"I hope he turns himself in soon. Despite what he did to me, he's my brother, and I wouldn't want to see him hurt," Shirlene muttered.

Bonnie turned to her with a concerned expression and asked, "Did you always know you were adopted?"

"Oh yeah, my parents told me at 18. They didn't want to have any secrets between us. It was a sealed adoption, and I never knew my actual parents."

"Do you think Sergio's father was waiting until your adoptive parents were deceased before sending this relic?" Bonnie continued, "Or did he just do it out of guilt?"

"Well, if he did, his timing is delayed by over a decade," Shirlene countered. "In my opinion, he definitely did it out of guilt from his deathbed."

"Well, we hear Isabella was a lovely person, although we know little about the man she conceived with," I added.

Shirlene shrugged her shoulders as if she didn't care and began reminiscing about the father that raised her. He was apparently a hard worker and a good provider for her and her mother, and very supportive of her as a child. He was also a stern disciplinarian and did not believe in showing a lot of emotions, and Shirlene believed that is how she formed such a tough exterior.

"Well, I, for one, admire that tough exterior. A toast to Shirlene and her tough exterior!" John exclaimed.

We all raised our glasses in a toast to Shirlene and quickly resumed eating our Torrone.

"On another note, I don't think you have anything to worry about regarding Sergio, but I am glad we upgraded your security system. I'm sorry the department couldn't assign you a security detail, but the budget has been really tight... or so I heard."

"That's okay, John, not everyone can be as lucky as Anna, and have a policeman living _in_ the home," Shirlene said jokingly.

"And exactly when can we expect the welcome mat to finally read 'Solace' versus 'Romano' you two lovebirds?" Bonnie questioned with raised eyebrows.

John jumped right in and offered, "I don't think there's any rush for now, but I have been considering a honeymoon in England. How about it, Anna?"

Shirlene and I both looked at each other in shock, then bust out laughing! We did not want to see England for many years.

"Okay, well, how about Paris? That's romantic. Or even Italy? Or a Caribbean island somewhere? You know, anywhere but Jersey is fine with me, rosebud."

"Seems like you're putting the cart before the horse, if you ask me!" Shirlene barked with a sarcastic tone. "You have to actually get married first, before you honeymoon."

John and I simply looked at each other and laughed just as his phone rang again. It was his parents, no doubt, asking about a wedding date.

"Mom, Dad, you'll be happy to know we were just talking about honeymoon destinations!" he boasted proudly. "Yes, Mom, we get it. Cart before the horse, okay. Geez."

He finished the call in the other room while us girls crowded around Bonnie to look at the latest pictures of the toddler, who is now apparently walking and talking, and the newest addition, who was only a few months old and apparently teething. And I thought my babies grew up fast!

| CHAPTER 12

Promises of Peace and Pastry Cream Delights

John

Now that the dust has settled and things were kind of back to normal, Billings and I are on another case of murder. A body was found near the Delaware River, wrapped in some type of rug. We were both thinking mafia, but who knows? The Feds wanted the case, and I agreed.

I was at my desk typing up the initial report and eating a spoonful of leftover Italian Chocolate Pastry Cream from the other night when my laptop started ringing. It was a video call from the Cambridgeshire Constabulary. I wiped my mouth of traces of chocolate and pressed the green phone icon. Chief Inspector Taylor and Constable Fernsby appeared on the screen, sitting at a table in the conference room.

"Great news, Detective Solace. We just arrested Sergio, without incident, trying to visit his aunt at the nursing home. Whether he was visiting or trying to keep her quiet is unknown; but either way, he will be tried for his crime of kidnapping and conspiracy to cause bodily harm, along with Ernesto, and ultimately convicted. Unless you plan on extraditing?"

"That is great news! And, no, we will not be extraditing. You are free to prosecute. I already got the okay from my captain and the DA."

"Can you inform Miss Booker for us?"

"Of course, I'm sure Shirlene will be happy to know he has been caught."

"I'm sure she will be, yes. She was hoping he would be taken into custody without incident, too."

"Indeed. And one more thing. As promised, we are delivering the other half of the relic. I hope it helps your friend to find peace."

"More great news. Thanks so much CI Taylor. We couldn't have solved this case without you and your men. Including you, Constable Fernsby!"

Constable just nodded his head, showing no emotion. Always one hundred percent professional.

"Before we hang up, I just have one question about Sergio's inheritance," I said hesitantly. "What happens if he is sentenced to life? Where does all of that go? Or, who does it go to, may be a better question?"

This time Constable Fernsby stepped in. "If I may, sir?"

CI Taylor waved his hand with his palm open as if giving him the floor and nodded.

"Thank you, sir. So, it all depends on the court ruling in his trial. If the judge gives him a life sentence and Ricardo Wright's final will stands, your friend, Miss Booker, inherits everything. Sergio never married, or had kids, and there are no other siblings that we know of."

"Wow," I said in amazement. "That would be incredible."

"Indeed, it would. We are talking about an estimated 72 billion dollar estate."

Still in awe, I thanked both of them again and signed off.

Next, I texted Anna to let her know the good news and asked her to tell Shirlene her half of the relic would be here soon. I kept the last part of my conversation to myself... for now.

"Billings, Solace, in my office!" the Captain summoned from the fishbowl.

I hurried into his office and let him know Billings was out to lunch. I didn't tell him it was with Putnam or that he had left two hours ago.

"How's the initial report coming on the DB in the rug?"

"Almost done, Captain. The Feds will have it within the hour."

"Well, we're gonna need it sooner than that. Gentlemen?"

Wondering who the captain was speaking to, I turned toward the doorway and two suits were staring at me.

"Come in and have a seat, please. We were just finishing up the paperwork, fellas. John, you remember our colleagues from your brother's case, right?"

I nodded and excused myself to finish the report, trying not to think about Scott. It was almost a year since his death and I still think about him often. Stuff from our childhood, the mess we got ourselves into as young adults, and the moments leading up to his death.

I stood up to grab some paper for the printer and noticed the blinds were closed and the door was shut in the captain's office. There seemed to be some heavy whispering back and forth going on, along with plenty of exaggerated hand gestures.

Twenty minutes later, I knocked on the door and handed them the paperwork and all the files I had on the case.

They looked at me as if they were forgetting something, said thanks, and left.

Why are the Feds always so strange and mysterious? It must be part of their MO.

"Did I miss anything, sir?"

It was Billings. He must have snuck in through the interrogation exit out back.

"No, just the Feds picking up the report on the possible mafia case. They were acting strange, as usual."

"I swear that must be on the job application for those guys. 'Must be able to appear mysterious at a moment's notice and constantly keep people guessing and in the dark'."

We both laughed while refilling our mugs with the precinct's interpretation of coffee. Even with a quarter cup of creamer, the black sludge showed no improvement. Ugh.

Billings was getting a call and ran back to his desk. When he picked up, his face changed. After a few 'uh-huhs' and 'you're kiddings', he hung up.

I looked at him perplexed and he tells me a neighbor of mine reported a dark sedan outside the house and that a male figure tried to break into the upstairs apartment.

"I'm sure Anna is okay, sir."

"Oh, she is. She was headed to Freehold to see Shirlene today."

We both grabbed our coats and keys and dashed to the car. Hopefully, we can lift some prints to identify this guy, and find out what the heck is going on.

CHAPTER 13

Wedding Bells at the Jersey Shore and Flannel Pajamas

Anna

I was trekking down the New Jersey Turnpike singing along to an old Hall and Oates song when my phone rang. It was John.

"Hi sweetie, what's going on?"

"Where are you?"

"About a mile away from getting onto the Garden State Parkway towards Freehold."

"Okay, good. There was a suspicious sedan seen outside the house and Billings and I are headed over to check it out."

"Our house? Well, that's strange. Just sitting outside? Let me guess, Mr. Craigly called it in, thinking it was suspicious."

"It was a female, so maybe his partner in crime called it in. They said a male figure tried to get into the upstairs apartment."

"What?! Well, thank goodness I wasn't home. Geez. Are my babies okay? What's happening to that community?" said the 'detective author' who brought police and dead bodies to her home only a year ago. I laughed to myself and realized I had completely tuned John out for a sec.

"Anna, you still there? I asked you a very serious question."

"Yes, sweetie, what was your question again?"

When he repeated the question, I was both shocked and appalled.

"Detective John Solace, I am NOT going to the Jersey Shore for our honeymoon!" I explained. Usually, when I use his full name, he knows I mean business, but not today.

"Why not?! A beach is a beach, right?"

"Hold on one sec while I pay this toll." I threw the quarters so harshly, I was expecting their return by bouncing off the plastic and onto the ground, but they swished downward and the light turned green.

"Okay, I'm back. Now, where was I?... Oh, yes. Just any beach is NOT acceptable. And I can't keep leaving my babies for weeks on end to gallivant across the country!"

"Two things. First of all, it's not gallivanting, it's our honeymoon, and the Jersey Shore is not in another country; and second, Billings and Putnam said they would stop in daily to check on them."

"I tell you what, how about five days in Florida?"

"Florida? Anna! You know how much I hate the humidity."

I could hear Billings laughing in the background.

"Please John. For me?"

"Okay, make it a nice, quiet beach resort—one not made for large families—and you have a deal."

"It's a deal! Now, my exit is coming up, dear. Anything else?"

"Actually, yes, I have some good news."

John proceeded to tell me all about his call with Chief Inspector Taylor and Constable Fernsby. I was speechless. I told him I would call in a little while after my visit with Shirlene.

When I pulled into Shirlene's driveway, I sat for a moment wondering how what John told me would change her life. Heck, it would change anybody's life. Would she still want to work? Would I need to find another publicist? Or publishing company?

There was a tap on my window.

Planes, Trains, and Relics of the Past

A man in plaid pajamas and matching slippers was waving hello profusely. I remembered him from my arrest for 'breaking and entering' into Shirlene's home. However, it was early afternoon, so the attire caught me off guard.

I waved and said hello as I exited the car, grabbing my purse and lunch tray from the front seat.

"Nice to see you again! Are you here to see Shirlene?"

He was smiling from ear to ear.

"Yes, I am. How are you, mister …?"

"Flannigan! Mr. Flannigan at your service! Shirlene is home, so you don't have to break in this time."

A name to match his attire. Interesting. "Yes, thank you," I replied.

"I'm also a big mystery buff. I work security down at the mall, and you would be surprised what I see on a daily basis. Anytime you want to brainstorm, I'm available. I have all my notes about the crimes neatly typed on index cards pinned to my corkboard in the basement. If you want, I can take you…"

"Boy, look at the time. Shirlene must be worried sick. I'll keep you in mind for sure, Mr. Flannigan. Bye for now!"

I rushed off and knocked on Shirlene's door like my life depended on it.

She opened the door as if she knew what I was 'running from'. I stepped in quickly, waving to her neighbor still standing by my car.

"I see you've met Mr. Flannigan and his flannel PJs," she roared.

"What a character. But, he is a fan, so I tried to be polite. How are you feeling?"

Shirlene took my hand and led me to the couch. She swallowed hard before she began speaking.

"Words cannot express how grateful I am to Constable Fernsby for helping me find out what he could about my birth father. I honestly wanted to forget, but I just couldn't let it go."

"I can understand that."

"We spoke, you know."

"To your birth father? Wow, Shirlene! How did that conversation go?"

"Better than expected. He didn't know Isabella had passed, and he never asked what happened to the child."

She went on to explain that he and his wife had a boy and a girl and they were all living in London. Since his health had started to decline, his daughter- and son-in-law offered to take him into their home. He suggested Shirlene come to visit and meet her half brother and sister one day, but I think Sergio made her hesitant about entertaining that idea.

There was a natural pause in the conversation, and I told her about the update on the case and that the relic was hers to keep.

She was stunned and began crying.

"I hope those are tears of joy! You're going to be an heiress. And a very wealthy one at that!" After a brief pause, I asked her if she would quit her career.

"I don't know what I would do without you," I said.

"I'm not going anywhere, Anna dear. But, boy, is it nice to know that cushion is there if me and my family, *both new and old*, need it."

We hugged and headed to the kitchen for lunch. I brought a platter of lunch meats and Italian rolls with fresh chocolate almond biscotti, while she put a pot of coffee on. It was going to be a long afternoon and a longer ride home.

| CHAPTER 14

911 and a Partial Print to Boot

John

Me and Billings pulled up to the house only to find Mr. Craigly and Ms. Martinez ready to greet us. Ms. Martinez was holding a small notebook and pencil. This was going to be a long afternoon.

They approached us as soon as we got out of the car.

The first one to speak was cranky Craigly. "What took you so long? What did you stop for coffee and donuts?" he snarled. From my peripheral view, I could see Billings was smirking, trying not to laugh.

I ignored the sarcasm, albeit we did stop for coffee, and turned to question Ms. Martinez.

"You called it in, Ms. Martinez?"

"Yes. Myself and Mr. Craigly take our jobs on the Neighborhood Watch committee VERY serious."

"Yes, I know you do, and we appreciate it. What did you see?"

"As I told the 911 operator, it was a dark sedan, no plates, and tinted windows. A slim man, maybe about your height, in all black clothing, walked right up the stairs to your garage apartment and began trying the door to see if he could get in."

"That's when I stepped in! I yelled out, 'Hey, you there? What are you doing?"

Mr. Craigly was gesturing wildly as he told his story.

"He was wearing one of those heavy sweatshirts that tie up over your head like the young kids today wear."

"You mean a hoodie, dear," said Ms. Martinez. "That's what they're calling it. Don't you remember?"

Trying to keep everyone on topic, I quickly asked, "And did he say anything at that point?"

"Nope, nothing! Coward! He probably knew about the bat I keep strapped to my chair! I would have clobbered him, too, but he took off in his fancy car!"

"Now, Arthur, you would have done no such thing. Calm yourself. Remember what the doctor said about your blood pressure?"

"Argh! What do they know? Blasted medical scammers. I'm going to lie down."

I called out a 'thank you' to Mr. Craigly, and Ms. Martinez followed closely after him. I'll have to remember to tell Anna I finally know his first name. Arthur.

"They're quite the pair, aren't they, sir?" Billings said.

"I'll say. I wonder why the perp didn't try the front door. What's the interest in the garage apartment?"

"I was thinking the same thing, sir. Oh, and here comes Carmen now."

I preferred Carmen over Victor, the "dude this and dude that" guy, any day. Carmen exited the van with her fingerprint kit in hand and a serious expression. All business as usual.

"Afternoon, detectives."

"Thanks for coming so quickly."

"Well, I was in Hamilton anyway at a bomb scare downtown, and headed back to the morgue to see Doc Bernstein."

"I haven't seen much of him lately. Tell him Solace says hello."

"I sure will. Which door did the perp touch?"

"The door above the garage."

She proceeded up the steps to take care of the task at hand.

Billings and I had the same idea. He pulled out his cellphone to check in on Putnam, while I called Anna.

I heard giggling at first, and then a female voice, but it was not Anna. "Hi John! So, a Florida wedding and honeymoon, huh?!"

"Well, just the … nevermind, yes, it looks that way Shirlene." I continued, "And, it looks like you may be a very wealthy bachelorette soon, huh?"

"I guess. I don't much care for the wealth, but I am excited about getting the relic back. Anyway, here's your darling Anna."

"Hey John. How's my handsome detective?"

"Okay. You two seem… happy."

"We are celebrating with the finest of red wine. Nothing like a little girl time, right?" she added.

"Not at all, rosebud. Just remember, you have to drive home tonight. And, speaking of home, I wanted to ask you if you could think of a reason anyone would want to get into the garage apartment."

"I have no clue, dear. I don't even use it for storage. Especially since Tess, you know, and Scott…"

"I understand. Did you happen to find anything when you were cleaning up after all of that occurred?

There was a long pause on the other end of the phone.

"No, nothing," Anna finally replied.

"Okay, I'll talk to you soon. Looks like Carmen is done getting the prints."

That pause made me wonder. Was Anna hiding something?

"No luck on the prints, sir, just a few partials. But you'll be pleased with what I found. A single drop of blood on the door frame."

"That's great, Carmen!" Billings gushed.

"Well, that could be anyone's, either me or Anna. We were always nicking our fingers on the window frame on the door."

Unfortunately, this was one of the many items on my Honey Do List. Ugh.

"Looked fresh to me, sir, but I'll keep you posted."

We waved Carmen off and hopped in the car to drive back to the station and wait for the results.

CHAPTER 15

Red Wine and a Blast From the Past

Anna

After sleeping off most of the wine I had consumed with Shirlene, I made the drive back to Princeton early the next morning. Traffic was light on the parkway and turnpike, so it was stress free and I cruised home in less than 45 minutes.

I pulled into the driveway and only saw Bette in the window. John opened the door before I could pull out my key.

"Morning rosebud."

"Morning, hun. You're up early." I said, as I bent down to scoop up Petra, one of my American Shorthair cats. Normally, I was the one up at the crack of dawn, while John awoke around 7am.

"I didn't sleep well. You know I cannot sleep if you're not beside me."

"I'm sorry, John. I won't be drinking red wine anytime soon, that's for sure."

"Good. How's Shirlene doing?"

"She's doing good. I admire how well she is handling this whole mess. Learning about her biological father and all. Did you know she had a half brother and sister?"

"In addition to Sergio? Wow."

"Anyway, she didn't suspect a thing about the other matter."

"Oh good. I was just going to ask. You know how you get when you drink."

I rolled my eyes and nodded in agreement, remembering the time I almost spilled the beans to Bonnie about a surprise anniversary trip to Jamaica her husband was planning. Red wine was the culprit then as well.

I saw the look of concern on John's face and asked him what was wrong.

"You think they will all hate us?" John asked.

"Hate is such a strong word, John. They may be *slightly* upset at the most. Isn't our happiness what's important?"

"I do, Mrs. Solace."

Suddenly, John grabbed me in a passionate kiss and wrapped his arms around me tight. I've never felt safer in his arms.

That's when I told him, in the midst of our embrace, about the note I found in Scott's drawer.

"John, dear."

"Yes, Anna."

"I may know what someone may have been looking for in the garage apartment."

"What? I knew it! As soon as you hesitated, I knew it!"

"Calm down, John. I just did not want to bother you with trivial stuff. Your brother just passed away, and you were grieving."

"Tell me."

I told him how I was clearing out Scott's belongings from the apartment and as I was pulling the clothes from a drawer, an envelope fell out onto the floor, so I opened it and read the note inside. It said, "If anything happens to me, ask the FBI why they failed me."

"That's strange."

"That's what I thought. And the date written in the top corner was way before he started the side job with LOV."

"Son of a —!" John yelled.

I cut him off before he started turning red with anger. "John, calm down, please. It probably means nothing. Just a coincidence, that's all. Why don't I whip up some waffles with strawberries and whipped cream?"

The food angle usually works, but I could see the nervous tick in his eye starting up. Just then, his phone rang.

I was rubbing his back to calm him as he answered it.

There was a bit of 'Mm-hmm's', followed by "I promise, I won't," and then he disconnected.

I asked what was wrong, and he headed to the couch to sit down. Even Tiny knew when to leave him alone and retreated under the couch with the others.

"John, what's wrong?"

"That was Carmen. I'm sure it's nothing, but…"

"But what, John? You're scaring me."

"Well, the prints on the door were a bust. Just partials. But the blood where it looked like a nick on that one area of the pane —."

"You mean the area on the door I've been asking you to fix for months now?"

"Yes Anna. Well, there were common alleles to me, but not an exact match."

"So, Scott stayed in the room, and your father may have been up there too."

"Carmen is positive the blood is fresh."

"Well, that's ridiculous. Scott is gone. She must have made a mistake."

I sat down slowly, trying to process what this meant. Scott was dead. We buried him, for goodness' sake. And I saw the coroner roll him out to his van on the day of the shootout. Scott was shot!

"Anna, Carmen is the most efficient CSI I know. That's why I'm so confused and torn at the same time." He rubbed his temples and closed his eyes for a minute before getting up.

"Where are you going?"

"Into the office for some answers."

I followed him into the bedroom as he frantically opened and closed each drawer in search of socks. After getting dressed, he grabbed his gun, keys, and badge, kissed me so long, and headed out the door.

"John, promise me you won't do anything crazy."

"Just like I told Carmen, I won't."

TatorTot, the quietest of the bunch, was perched up on the screen door with her hind legs meowing. It's as if she could sense what was coming. The calm before the storm.

I headed back to the couch to call my mother and clear up all of her questions, as well as update her on Shirlene. She'll be happy to know she's okay and that she may soon be a very wealthy woman.

It's better to keep myself busy, versus worrying myself into a frenzy about John's next move.

Afterwards, I can catch up on my Dear Jesse column. Today, I'd rather deal with other people's problems than my own.

| CHAPTER 16

A Case in Question and a Body in Limbo

John

My mind was racing with a million questions as I headed to the precinct. What did the note mean? When and why did the FBI approach Scott in the first place? What weren't they telling me? Was the captain in on it? Was there some kind of coverup going on?

I couldn't think without caffeine, so I pulled into the parking lot of Twenty Volts Café for a quick fix. Luckily for me, the morning rush had passed. After a minute, I stepped up to the barista to order. It was a young man I hadn't seen before, with bright blue hair, green eyes, piercings on his nose and bottom lip, and an earring that was black, circular, and made his ear lobe look as if there was a huge hole in it. He spoke very low and monotone, as if half asleep, and annoyed I was bothering him.

"Good morning. My name is Brandon. Would you like to try our special, Caramel Crave Super Shocker, today?"

He sighed as if I was taking too long to decide, even though only a millisecond had passed.

"Sure, sounds great. Shock me."

By the eye roll, I assumed I was not as amusing as I thought, and swiped my card to pay and move to the next line to pickup my coffee.

"Sir! Your name?"

After spelling Solace three times, I finally got my coffee jolt, and one for my partner, and continued the five-minute drive to the office.

Billings had beaten me again; always the early bird. I placed the coffee on his desk.

"Thanks, sir. What's up for today?"

"Let's take a walk."

Billings knew what that meant. It was something private I did not want the 'ears' of the precinct to hear. He grabbed his jacket and followed me out the glass doors.

When we got halfway to the park at the end of the street, I spoke. I explained Carmen's findings, the note Anna found, the questions it raised, and asked for his thoughts.

"That's pretty suspicious, sir. If we didn't all see the body carried to the coroner's van, I would suspect foul play, but we did, sir. And Anna saw him get shot and go down."

"I know. It does sound ludicrous. But what if he made a deal with the Feds in exchange for them helping him 'disappear'? I mean, we didn't actually 'see' the body. Just the body bag."

"What could Scott possibly help them with, sir? I just can't fathom that scenario."

"Well, I'm going to do some digging. I need you to watch my back, okay?"

"Yeah, no problem, sir. Anything you need?"

We turned to head back to the office. I told Billings my suspicions about the meeting the other day between the suits and the Captain, and how he closed the blinds to the fishbowl—which was never a good sign.

Billings concurred. "Oh, well, we all know what that means. Serious business."

"Exactly."

"But it could have been about the mafia case, sir."

I nodded in agreement, rubbing my chin, thinking as we entered the building.

"Where have you two been?! You have a lead on an attempted murder case from a month ago!"

It was the captain, and he seemed to be in rare form.

"We're on it, sir!" Billings answered promptly. "Just getting some air, sir."

"Well, there's air in here! Follow up on the lead before they change their mind! Our close rate is not great this month, and the brass is all over me to get the numbers up!"

I tried to keep up with his pace and follow him back to his office while Billings was "Yes-sirring" him to death.

"Captain, you gotta minute?" I asked hurriedly.

"You got thirty seconds, Solace!" he shouted.

I followed him into the fishbowl, trying to figure out how to phrase my inquiry. I didn't wanna show all of my cards at once. If I look too paranoid, he'll send me home on a mental health day.

"Um, sir, was everything okay with the mafia case file? I noticed a lot of hush-hush when the Feds were here and just wanted to be sure, you know?"

"The file was fine, as far as I know. Is that all?"

"It's funny they were the exact suits that worked my brother's case, huh?" I released a strained laugh that sounded more like a cough.

The boss was not amused. It seemed all the lines on his forehead collapsed into the space between his eyebrows and he slowly tilted his head slightly.

"How is that funny? Are you purposely trying to upset me, Solace?"

"No, sir. Not ha-ha funny, just ironically funny."

After shaking my head "Nevermind", I headed back to my desk as quickly as possible. I'll have to go about this another way.

I started digging into the FBI database for anything related to Scott's case, but nothing came up. And, the one file I found was classified, and I didn't have the rank or security level to open it.

"Any luck, sir?" Billings asked.

I leaned on my desk, elbows first, with my head in my hands. "No, nothing. Not with the cap and not in the federal database."

"You'll find something, sir. Don't worry."

"Solace!"

Billings and I looked up at the slightly stocky, muscular male with the bald head, goatee, and beige jumpsuit looking around as he called out my name again. "Delivery for Solace!"

"Yeah, over here."

He was pushing a large moving cart with an even larger box.

"Hey, how ya doin'? I got a delivery from the customs office. Looks like it's from England. High security too, based on the level of 'protection'," he said as he raised one hand as a cover and pointed behind him with the other.

Billings and I had no idea what he was pointing to until an elderly male officer with wispy white hair came shuffling up behind him. Now I understand what the precinct meant by budget cuts.

"Follow me, gentleman. Let's get this to our secure lockup area," I said.

After everything was signed, sealed and delivered, I texted Anna to arrange for Shirlene to come up to the station to sign for everything.

I could tell she was excited by the number of exclamation points at the end of her 'Yay!' message. I told her I would 'be home by six' with a heart emoji.

Even though my mind was still on Scott, I turned my attention back to my caseload and improving the department's close rate, when an email came in that made me smile, and I'm sure will bring a smile to Shirlene's face. Looks like the trial judge is ruling in her favor after all.

CHAPTER 17

Jewels, Lies, and Parties on the Beach

Anna

"I'm sorry, Shirlene. I'm running late. Tiny wasn't feeling well this morning. I spent most of the day cleaning up his spit-up from the carpet."

"Oh no! Is he okay?"

"Well, the vet says it was something he ate, although I can't imagine what he got into. He gave him CERENIA to calm his stomach."

"Okay, well, I understand if you can't make it."

"Oh no, I wouldn't miss this for the world. I just need to drop Tiny off at home and I'll be along shortly."

At last I was out of the traffic jam on Route 1 and almost to my street. I pulled up to the curb to find Mr. Craigly lurking about. I put on a smile, grabbed Tiny from the back seat, and walked up to say hello.

"Everything okay, Mr. Craigly?"

"No, it is not okay. Carl Tippins did not show up for his shift today, and now I am stuck policing the street for the day _and_ evening shift."

"Oh, I see. Well, maybe he had an emergency. Did you call him?"

"I can't check up on everyone all the time, you know! What's in that thing?"

"You mean the carrier? This is Tiny, one of my cats."

"Ugh! Well, how many of those things do you have?"

"Only seven. And they are not things, they are the most adorable and personable animals. Tiny, Sonny, and Petra are my shorthairs, then TatorTot is my beautiful Persian, and —."

"Okay, I get it. I better move it along and make sure there are no more strange cars idling at the end of the street."

How rude. He was the one that asked about my babies.

"Come on Tiny. Let's get you inside. Mommy has an appointment to get to."

It was getting rather chilly. There must be a storm coming. I grabbed my sunflower rain jacket off the coat rack by the door and heading back out to meet everyone at the station.

* * *

"Hi Shirlene. Hello dear. Sorry I'm late, everyone," I said apologetically.

"How's Tiny? What did the vet say?"

I explained the diagnosis once again and confirmed to everyone he was fine.

"So, what have I missed?" I asked with excited curiosity.

Shirlene turned to me and took my hand. "Nothing. I wanted to wait for you. Without you, I couldn't imagine doing what I do."

Even though she was trying to put on a brave face for everyone, her hand was trembling.

Billings approached us and announced, "The room is ready, sir."

"Great, thanks. Ladies, this way, please." John said as he led the way with the wave of his hand.

John explained the precinct had a secure room inside the evidence room for reviewing and storing valuable items. I had never seen this part of the building, and Billings had to use his swipe card several times to get us through the various doors and levels of security.

We finally arrived in what looked like a metal cage, and then a sealed room inside that cage was where we ended up.

I dare think what would happen in the event of a fire, geez. The term 'sitting ducks' comes to mind.

We all sat down at the table while Billings rolled in a long brown box with various carvings on it. I could tell everyone was mouthing the same word as me. Wow.

I continued to hold Shirlene's hand for support.

Billings slid the box on the table, then unlocked and opened it. The interior of the box comprised the same engravings within the top, inner lid, but the bottom was encased in red felt. There was a mechanism that lifted into two drawers that seem to hold what seemed to be over fifty artifacts. There were gauntlets, rings, bowls with engravings, and so much more.

"What's all of this?" Shirlene inquired in awe.

"Holy cow. This really is a treasure," I muttered.

"The entire fortune is yours, Shirlene. By ruling of the trial judge. I was saving the news for today. Looks like Sergio will be locked up for a long time," John explained.

Everyone continued to stare in amazement as Shirlene reached for the artifact labeled with her name. It was her half of the Tristan's Corinthian Cross, sent to her by her stepfather, *for lack of a better term*. The fact that he sent her away at birth and had a change of heart on his deathbed meant nothing to her. For her, it meant he had continued to think of her all those years when she was growing up in the U.S.

"How much do you think this is worth?" Billings asked.

"Enough for Sergio to kill over, apparently," I said.

"Well, the appraiser in England told CI Taylor you could live off of it for the rest of your life, but that's only if you sold parts of it," John responded.

"Incredible," I uttered.

No one wanted to mention the elephant in the room, so I offered.

"Soooo, let's find the other half. You know what the professor said. Magical powers and all."

"You don't believe in all of that, do you?" We looked up to see Putnam leaning in the doorway with her arms folded and a sly grin on her face.

"Is there a reason I wasn't invited to the party?" she said with one eyebrow up. Her gaze was directed at Billings.

"Putnam, please, sit down! We were just about the examine the Tristan's Corinthian Cross," I said.

I was digging through the collection attempting to find the other half given to Sergio, when Shirlene raised her hand up slowly in awe. It was an ancient cross like her half, but everyone knew from the professor of its potential when both halves were connected.

Suddenly, the phone in the room rang. John picked it up and sounded surprised. He hung up and turned on the monitor in the room, then signed into the laptop and clicked a link.

"Hello, Professor! Nice to see you again."

Professor Henry Davies was on the big screen, front and center. With glasses on the edge of his nose, and his nose pressed so close to the screen, we could see a few nose hairs. His curly hair scattered in many directions on the top of his head. We knew how anxious he was by the lines in his forehead and wide, open eyes.

We all said hello and made the usual pleasantries.

"Did I miss it?" he asked.

"No, we were just about to make the connection."

"Ah, good. Carry on, please!"

Shirlene handed Sergio's half of the cross to me while she held the other half. We held them high above the table, so the professor could see. As we moved them closer, a strong magnetic connection pulled them together. Suddenly, there was a loud click.

A red glow radiated from the underside. We turned it over and there it was. The largest and brightest ruby I had ever seen.

"Absolutely bloody remarkable. The ruby was not even visible within the separate halves. Completely hidden until the two halves were joined," the professor muttered in astonishment.

We were all squinting from the glow of the gem and wondering what tales from the historic past this artifact could tell, if it could speak.

"If I may, if you have time, I would like to have an image of the carvings on the case to see if I can interpret them," the professor asked.

Shirlene quickly responded, "Of course, I would love to learn more about the history of all of this."

After we disconnected with the professor and finished our exploration, John had everything boxed back up and had a police escort, *meaning Putnam and Billings*, accompany her to the bank. Shirlene wanted everything in a safe deposit box for now until she figured out what to do with it. There were many collectors and museums that would pay top dollar for just one item from the collection.

* * *

Later, Shirlene and I were back at the house relaxing on the sofa with TaterTot in her lap purring, when she caught me off guard.

"Okay, fess up."

"What on earth are you talking about?"

"You know what, Anna. I'm talking about the two hour disappearing act in London and the unusual glow radiating from you and John. Brighter than my cross' ruby!"

"I really don't know what—"

Shirlene put up her hand to stop me and I put my head down as if to surrender. I stood up and went to the kitchen to fetch the Bicerin I was making. When I returned with the tray, I placed the two mugs down on the coffee table and said, "Okay, you win. But please promise you won't be upset with me."

"Just spill it, Anna. And I don't mean the coffee!"

"We did it."

"IT as in what? By the way, this Italian coffee is divine. Anyway, IT, as in what?"

"IT as in… um…" I couldn't say it, so I fiddled in my pocket for a second and my hand emerged with a ring on it.

"Holy Crap! Anna, you didn't?!"

"We did. We snuck off to St Pauls Cathedral in London, only a half hour from Madame Tussaud's by train, and made it official!"

"Gosh, I'm speechless. I mean, congratulations! But I'm still mad at you. I thought you wanted a small ceremony. What happened?"

"Nothing happened. It was John's idea, actually. And we simply stopped at a small jewelry shop for a small ring. And… we just did it."

"Wait, what about the whole Florida thing?"

"Actually, we wanted to invite all of you to come for our wedding reception celebration."

"Heck yeah, that's fabulous! Count me in! Just no boats or cruises!"

I told Shirlene it was a deal, and we both laughed and hugged.

I texted John the cat was out of bag and he spread the word to Billings and Putnam.

Me: Sorry, dear. Our glow gave it away. See you at home for dinner, Mr. Solace.

John: See you at home, Mrs. Solace.

Life is good. My best friend was safe, my babies were okay, I was married to my handsome detective, and doing a job I love, writing mysteries. All of this joy made me forget about this horrible nonsense over Scott's death. My mind was racing. I had temporarily tuned out Shirlene rambling on about hotels on the beach for the reception venue.

I was too busy thinking of a title for my next book, *Witness Protection*.

About the Author

Cheryl Denise Bannerman is an award-winning, multi-genre author of nine published works of fiction – from murder mysteries to a recent children's book about friendship.

She is the winner of the 2018 Book Excellence Award for her book of poetry, *Words Never Spoken*, and winner of the Best Books Awards in the category of African American fiction in 2020 and winner of the Reader's Favorite 2021 International Book Award Contest in the Urban Fiction category for *Black Child to Black Woman*. She is also a Semi-Finalist in the MLC Audiobook Awards with a 2020 IMDb Nomination for Book 1 of the Anna Romano Mystery Series, *Cats, Cannolis, and a Curious Kidnapping*.

The author draws her inspiration from life experiences, observations, and lessons. Her goal in life is to keep writing and continue helping victims of Domestic Abuse/Violence, Grief, and ANON family groups, and Corporate Health and Wellness groups, to heal through words — encouraging them to 'write the pain' via journaling, and expressing themselves through short stories, songs, and poetry.

When she is not working from her home office on her virtual Training and Development business, she is at the beach watching the waves and weaving the words together for her next novel.

Check out some of her other works of fiction at www.bannermanbooks.com

Appendix of Tasty Recipes

Pasta Fagioli Soup

TOTAL TIME: Prep/Total Time: 30 min.
YIELD: 5 servings.

INGREDIENTS

- 1/2 pound Italian turkey sausage links, casings removed, crumbled
- 1 small onion, chopped
- 1-1/2 teaspoons canola oil
- 1 garlic clove, minced
- 2 cups water
- 1 can (15-1/2 ounces) great northern beans, rinsed and drained
- 1 can (14-1/2 ounces) diced tomatoes, undrained
- 1 can (14-1/2 ounces) reduced-sodium chicken broth
- 3/4 cup uncooked elbow macaroni
- 1/4 teaspoon pepper
- 1 cup fresh spinach leaves, cut as desired
- 5 teaspoons shredded Parmesan cheese

DIRECTIONS

1. In a large saucepan, cook sausage over medium heat until no longer pink; drain, remove from pan and set aside. In the

same pan, saute onion in oil until tender. Add garlic; saute 1 minute longer.

2. Add the water, beans, tomatoes, broth, macaroni, and pepper; bring to a boil. Cook, uncovered, until macaroni is tender, 8-10 minutes.

3. Reduce heat to low; stir in sausage and spinach. Cook until spinach is wilted, 2-3 minutes. Garnish with cheese.

Resource: https://www.tasteofhome.com/collection/recipes-for-old-world-italian-food/

Linguine with White Clam Sauce

Level: Easy
Total: 35 min
Active: 20 min
Yield: 4 to 6 servings

INGREDIENTS

1 pound dry linguine or spaghetti

Kosher salt

1/3 cup extra-virgin olive oil

3 tablespoons finely chopped garlic

1/2 teaspoon red pepper flakes

3/4 cup dry white wine

1/4 cup water

36 little neck clams, scrubbed

3 tablespoons finely chopped flat-leaf parsley

Freshly ground pepper

Grilled bread, for serving (optional)

DIRECTIONS

Bring a large pot of water to a boil and season generously with salt. Boil the pasta until al dente, tender but still firm.

While the pasta cooks make the clam sauce. Heat the olive oil in a large saute pan over medium-low heat. Add the garlic and cook until softened but not browned, about 3 minutes. Add the pepper flakes and cook for 30 seconds more. Add the wine and water and increase the heat to high. Add the clams, cover, and cook, shaking the pan periodically, until all the clams are opened, about 6 minutes.

Drain the pasta and add to the clam sauce. Add the parsley and toss to combine. Season with salt and pepper to taste. Divide among heated bowls and serve immediately.

To prepare the grilled bread, pre-heat a grill pan over medium heat. Brush the bread with olive oil on both sides. Grill until toasted, 1 to 2 minutes per side.

Resource: https://www.foodnetwork.com/recipes/food-network-kitchen/linguine-with-white-clam-sauce-recipe-2011623

Chocolate Torrone

Prep time: 20 mins

Cook time: 20 mins

Chilling time: 3 hrs

Total time: 3 hrs 40 mins

INGREDIENTS FOR COATING

  12.3 ounces dark chocolate (good quality) (350 grams)

INGREDIENTS FOR FILLING:

  5.3 ounces milk chocolate (150 grams)

  3.5 ounces white chocolate (100 grams)

  3.5 ounces dark chocolate (100 grams)

  1/2 cup Nutella (150 grams)

  1 3/4 - 2 cups hazelnuts (whole peeled and toasted) (235 grams)

DIRECTIONS FOR COATING

On low heat, place the coating chocolate (broken into pieces) in a medium bowl over a pot of water (make sure the bowl does not touch the water). Melt until smooth, stirring often with a spatula or whisk. Remove from heat and coat a silicone loaf pan 8.5 x 4.5 inch (22 x 11 cm), or a parchment paper lined loaf pan. Swirling or brushing the chocolate to coat evenly, drain any extra chocolate back into the bowl. Freeze the loaf pan for about 10-15 minutes or until hardens, coat one more time and freeze again for 10 minutes. Use the remaining chocolate for the topping.

FILLING

While the coating is in the freezer, melt together the milk, white, and dark chocolate the same way as above. Once it is melted, remove from the heat and stir in the Nutella, continue stirring until smooth. Fold in the hazelnuts, remove the loaf pan from the freezer and add the hazelnut filling. Refrigerate for approximately 30 minutes. Remove from the fridge and cover with the remaining dark chocolate coating. Cover lightly with foil and refrigerate 3-6 hours. Remove from loaf pan and slice or chop into pieces.

NOTES

If the Torrone becomes quite hard after being in the fridge, it might be best to let it sit for approximately 15 minutes before slicing, although I chopped it in large pieces instead.

If you buy untoasted hazelnuts, then you can either place the hazelnuts in a large frying pan and heat on medium heat for approximately 2 minutes stirring occasionally, then remove from pan and let cool. Or bake in a pre-heated 350°F oven for 5 - 7 minutes. Just be sure to remove them from the pan to a bowl so they don't continue to bake.

Torrone can be stored in the freezer for up to six months.

Substitution: You can substitute Nutella with less than half a cup of sweetened condensed milk.

Resource: https://anitalianinmykitchen.com/chocolate-torrone/#recipe

Cheryl Denise Bannerman

Chocolate Almond Biscotti

Biscotti (/bɪˈskɒti/; **Italian** pronunciation: [biˈskɔtti]; English: biscuits), known also as cantucci ([kanˈtuttʃi]), are **Italian** almond biscuits that originated in the Tuscan city of Prato. They are twice-baked, oblong-shaped, dry, crunchy, and may be dipped in a drink, traditionally Vin Santo.

Prep time: 15 mins

Cook time: 25 mins

Total time: 40 mins

INGREDIENTS

   3/4 cup whole skinned almonds

   2 eggs

   3/4 cup sugar

   1 3/4 cup + 2 tablespoons all purpose flour

   2 tablespoons cocoa

   1/4 teaspoon salt

   1 teaspoon baking powder

   1 1/2 teaspoons honey

   1 teaspoon vanilla

   zest from 1/2 orange

   3 1/2 ounces dark chocolate (good quality)

Planes, Trains, and Relics of the Past

DIRECTIONS

1. Pre-heat oven to 350°. Line a cookie sheet with parchment paper.

2. On an unlined cookie sheet toast almonds for approximately 5 minutes in the pre-heated oven. Remove from oven, move to a small bowl and let cool.

3. In a medium bowl, beat eggs and sugar to combine, then add flour, cocoa, salt, baking powder, honey, vanilla, and zest and combine with a wooden spoon, then fold in the almonds.

4. Move to a lightly floured flat surface and gently knead into a soft dough.

5. Divide into 2-3 parts and form into 2-3 logs (I found 3 logs to be just right). Approximately 8-10 inches long, place on prepared cookie sheet and brush with beaten egg (a small egg). Bake for approximately 20 minutes.

6. Remove from oven, let sit 5 minutes and then cut each log into 1/4 inch slices on the diagonal, place cut side up on the cookie sheet and bake again for approximately 5-10 minutes or until dry. Let cool completely before dipping in melted chocolate. Yields about 30 cookies. Enjoy!

Resource: https://anitalianinmykitchen.com/chocolate-almond-biscotti/

Italian Coffee Recipe (also known as Bicerin)

INGREDIENTS

½ cup strong coffee

½ cup hot chocolate

¼ cup heavy cream

Chocolate shavings optional

DIRECTIONS

Put a mason jar in the freezer (this is for making the cream topping. If you'd rather use whipped cream, skip this step).

Make a pot of strong coffee.

While the coffee is brewing, make yourself a batch of hot chocolate. We recommend something homemade and creamy, but any hot chocolate will work.

Pour your hot chocolate into the bottom one third of your mug.

Pour your coffee over the back of a spoon into the mug, filling to two-thirds full.

Put your heavy cream into the chilled mason jar and close.

Shake until the cream thickens slightly.

Pour cream over the back of a spoon, filling the mug completely.

Top with chocolate shavings.

Resource: https://www.nelliebellie.com/italian-coffee-recipe/

What Did You Think of Planes, Trains, and Relics of the Past?

First, thank you for purchasing the fourth book in The Anna Romano Murder Mystery Series, **Planes, Trains, and Relics of the Past**. I know you could have picked any number of books to read, but you picked this book, and for that, I am extremely grateful.

I hope it added value and quality to your everyday life. If so, it would be awesome if you could share this book with your friends and family by posting to social media.

If you enjoyed this book and found some benefit in reading this, I would like to hear from you and hope that you could take some time to post a review online. Your feedback and support will help me improve my writing craft for future projects and make this book even better.

Visit the website at www.bannermanbooks.com for contact information.

I want you, the reader, to know that your opinion is very important to me and hope that you will check out my other works of fiction:

Title	Category/Genre
Cats, Cannolis, and a Curious Kidnapping	Book 1 of the Anna Romano Mystery Series
A Bloody Stiletto, Cold Lasagna, and a Bestseller	Book 2 of the Anna Romano Mystery Series
Family Ties, Missing Organs, & Champagne	Book 3 of the Anna Romano Mystery Series
Words Never Spoken	Women's Inspirational/Poetry
A Killer's Reflection	Erotic Psychological Thriller/Serial Killer
Black Child to Black Woman	Women's Fiction/Urban Fiction/Family Saga
Black Child to Black Woman Journal	Self-help
The Gecko Without an Echo	Children's Illustrated Rhyming